Dear Reader,

My name's Brand St. Clair, but trust me—I'm no saint. I'm a bush pilot in Alaska and I'm considered something of a daredevil. A few years back I was devastated when my wife died. I loved Sandra and never expected to love another woman. That's what shook me so badly when I met Carly. I liked her immediately, and I don't mind telling you that she scared the living daylights out of me.

Once several years back I came face-to-face with a bear, but Carly terrified me more because I knew I was going to love this woman with all my heart. I have to tell you, Carly's a bit stubborn, but once you get to know her, you'll forgive her for that. I know I did!

Brand St. Clair

DEBBIE MACOMBER

Borrowed Dreams

Alaska

Published by Silhouette Books New York

America's Publisher of Contemporary Romance

SILHOUETTE BOOKS
300 East 42nd St., New York, N.Y. 10017

BORROWED DREAMS

ISBN: 0-373-45152-0

Published Silhouette Books 1985, 1993

All the characters in this book have no existence outside the
imagination of the author and have no relation whatsoever to
anyone bearing the same name or names. They are not even
distantly inspired by any individual known or unknown to the
author, and all incidents are pure invention.

® and ™ are trademarks used under license. Trademarks recorded
with ® are registered in the United States Patent and Trademark
Office, the Canadian Trade Marks Office and in other countries.

Printed in the U.S.A.

Chapter One

"Don't worry about a thing," George Hamlyn stated casually on his way out the door.

"Yes...but—" Carly Grieves interrupted.

"Take any phone messages and straighten the place up a bit. That should keep you busy for the day." He removed his faded cap and wiped his forearm across his wide brow as he paused just inside the open doorway.

All day! Carly mused irritably. "What time should I expect you back?"

"Not until afternoon at the earliest. I'm late now." His voice was tinged with accusation. "A couple of drivers will be checking in soon. They have their instructions."

Fleetingly, Carly wondered if their orders were as vague as her own.

"See you later." George tossed her a half smile and was out the door before Carly could form another protest.

Carly dropped both hands lifelessly to her sides in frustrated displeasure. How could George possibly expect her to manage the entire office on her own? But, apparently, he did just that. On her first day, no less. With only a minimum of instruction, she was to take over the management of Alaska Freight Forwarding in her employer's absence.

"Didn't Diana warn you this would happen?" She spoke out loud, standing in the middle of the room, feeling hopelessly inadequate. Good heavens, what had she gotten herself into with this job?

Hands on hips, Carly surveyed the room's messy interior. George had explained, apologetically, that his last traffic supervisor had left three months ago. One look at the office confirmed his statement. How could anyone run a profitable business in such chaos? The long counter was covered with order forms and a variety of correspondence, some stained with dried coffee; the ashtray that sat at one end was filled to overflowing. Cardboard boxes littered the floor, some stacked as high as the ceiling. The two desks were a disaster; a second full ashtray rested in the center of hers, on top of stacked papers, and empty coffee mugs littered its once polished wood surface. The air was heavy with the smell of stale tobacco.

Forcefully expelling an uneven sigh, Carly paused and wound a strand of rich brown hair around her ear.

Straighten the place up a bit! her mind mimicked George's words. She hadn't come all the way from Seattle to clean offices. Her title was traffic supervisor, not janitor!

Annoyed with herself for letting George walk all over her, Carly got her desk in reasonable order and straightened the papers on the counter. She grimaced as she examined the inside of the coffeepot. It looked as if it had never been washed.

When the phone rang, she answered in a brisk, professional tone. "Alaska Freight Forwarding."

A short hesitation followed. "Who's this?"

Squaring her shoulders, she replied crisply. "Carly Grieves. May I ask who's calling?"

The man at the other end of the line ignored the question. "Let me talk to George."

It seemed no one in Alaska had manners. "George is out for the day. May I ask who's calling?"

"Dammit." The low words were issued with a vengeance.

"I beg your pardon?"

"When do you expect him back?"

"Well, Mr. Dammit, I can't rightly say." Carly couldn't resist christening him with his own words.

"I'll be there in ten minutes." With that, he abruptly severed their connection.

Sighing, Carly replaced the receiver. Apparently Mr. Dammit thought she could tell him something more in person.

A few minutes later, the door burst open and a man as lean and serious as an arctic wolf strode briskly inside and stopped just short of the counter. Dark flecks sparked with interest in eyes that were wide and deeply set. He was dressed in a faded jean jacket and worn jeans, and his Western-style, checkered shirt was open at the throat to reveal a broad chest with a sprinkling of curly, dark hair.

"Carly Grieves?" he questioned as his mouth quirked into a coaxing smile.

"Mr. Dammit?" she returned, and couldn't restrain the involuntary smile that tugged at the edges of her soft mouth. His lean face was tanned from exposure to the elements. The dark, wind-tossed hair was indifferent to any style. This man was earthy and perhaps a little wild—the kind of wild that immediately gave women the desire to tame. Carly was no exception.

"Brand St. Clair," he murmured, his friendly eyes not leaving hers as he extended his hand.

Her own much smaller hand was enveloped in his callused, roughened one. "I'm taking a truck," he announced without preamble.

"You're what?" Carly blinked.

"I haven't got time to explain. Tell George I was by—he'll understand."

"I can't let you do that ... I don't think ..." Carly stammered, not knowing what to do. Brand St. Clair wasn't on the clipboard that listed Alaska Freight Forwarding employees. What if one of the men from the warehouse needed a truck later? She didn't know this man. True, he was strikingly attractive, but he'd undoubtedly used that to his advantage more than once. "I can't let you do that," she decided firmly, her voice gaining strength.

Brand smiled, but the amusement didn't touch his dusky, dark eyes. Despite the casual way he was leaning against the counter, Carly recognized that he was tense and alert. The thought came that this man was deceptive. For all his good looks and charming smile, it could be unwise to cross him.

"I apologize if this is inconvenient," she began, and clasped her hands together with determination. "But I've only just started this job. I don't know you. I don't know if George Hamlyn is in the habit of lending out his trucks, and furthermore . . ."

"I'll accept full responsibility." He took his wallet from his back hip pocket and withdrew a business card, handing it to her.

Carly read the small print. Brand was a pilot who free-lanced his services to freight operators.

"A hiker in Denali Park has been injured," he explained shortly. "I'm meeting the park rangers and airlifting him to British Columbia." The clipped, impatient way he spoke told Carly he wasn't accustomed to making explanations.

"I . . . I . . ." Carly paused, uncertain.

"Do I get the truck or not?"

She unclenched and clenched her fist again. "All right," she finally conceded, and handed over the set of keys.

He gave her a brief salute and was out the door.

She stood at the wide front window that faced the street and watched as Brand backed the pickup truck onto the road, changed gears and sped out of sight. Shrugging one shoulder, she arched two delicate brows expressively. Life in the north could certainly be unnerving.

"A pilot," she murmured. Flying was something that had intrigued her from childhood. The idea of soaring thousands of feet above the earth with only a humming engine keeping her aloft produced a thrill of adventure. Carly wondered fleetingly if she'd get the opportunity to learn to fly while in Alaska.

She paused, continuing to stand at the window. Her attraction to the rugged stranger surprised her. She preferred her men tame and uncomplicated, but something about Brand St. Clair had aroused her curiosity. She couldn't put her finger on it now, but it was as real and intense as anything she'd ever experienced. It could have been that animal magnetism that exuded from him or his latent sensuality, but Carly doubted it. She'd been exposed to those male qualities a hundred times and had walked away yawning. But whatever it was, Carly found that she was affected by their short encounter and she stood watching the road long after the truck was out of sight.

Once the formica counter was cleaned, the orders piled in neat stacks, and the boxes pushed to one side of the office, Carly took a short cigarette break. She glared at the glowing tip of the cigarette and directed a long puff of smoke at the ceiling. Cutting back on the bad habit would be easier once she was settled in.

A few minutes later, as she ground out the butt in the clean ashtray, she wondered why she continued to kid herself. Five years of a bad habit weren't going to be easily wiped out just because she'd moved north.

The phone rang several times and Carly wrote down the messages dutifully, placing them on George's desk. A warehouse man came in and introduced himself before lunch, but was gone before Carly could question him about the truck Brand St. Clair had taken.

With time on her hands the afternoon dragged, and Carly busied herself by sorting through the filing cabinets. If the office was in disarray, it was nothing compared to the haphazard methods George employed for filing.

When George sauntered in around five he stopped in the doorway and glanced around before giving Carly an approving nod.

"I'd like to talk to you a minute," she informed him stiffly. She wasn't beyond admitting she'd made a mistake, cutting her losses and heading back to Seattle. If he needed someone to clean house, she wasn't it.

"Sure." He shrugged and sat down at his desk. Although George possessed a full head of white hair, he didn't look more than fifty. Guessing his age was difficult, because George's eyes were sparkling with life and vitality. "What can I do for you?" he asked as he rolled back his chair and casually rested an ankle on top of his knee.

Carly remained standing. "First off, I'm a freight traffic supervisor. I didn't cart everything I own a thousand miles to clean your coffeepot or anything else.''

''That's fine.'' George's smile was absent as he shuffled through the phone messages. ''Contact a janitorial service. I've been meaning to do that myself.''

His assurance took some of the steam from her anger. ''And another thing. Brand St. Clair was in and took...*borrowed* a truck. He said it was an emergency and I wasn't sure if I should've stopped him.''

''No problem.'' George glanced up, looking mildly surprised. His thoughts seemed to have drifted a thousand miles from her indignation. ''One of these days that boy will come to his senses and give it up.''

'''Give it up'?'' Carly repeated, amused that she had verbalized her thought.

George nodded, then set the mail aside. ''I've been after Brand to join up with us. He's a damn good pilot.'' His eyes moved to Carly and he lifted one shoulder in an indifferent shrug. ''Not likely, though, with all those medical bills he's paying off. He can earn twice the money free-lancing.''

''Medical bills?'' Carly voiced her curiosity.

George appeared not to have heard her question. ''Any other problems?''

''Not really.''

He shook his head, his eyes drifting to the stack of mail. ''I'll see you in the morning then.''

There was no mistaking the dismissal in his tone. Already he had turned his attention to the desk.

Carly left the office shortly afterward, wondering how much longer George would be staying. The man was apparently married to his job. There was little evidence in the office that he had a wife and family. And the hours he seemed to keep would prohibit any kind of life outside the company.

The apartment Carly had rented on Weimer Drive was a plain one-bedroom place that was barely large enough to hold all her furniture. Some of her things were being shipped from Seattle and wouldn't arrive for another month. Diana—dear, sweet, Diana—couldn't believe that Carly would give up a good job in comfortable surroundings on the basis of a few phone conversations with George Hamlyn from the parent company. Her friend was convinced Carly was running. But she wasn't. Alaska offered adventure, and she'd been ready for a change.

Hugging her legs, her chin resting on a bent knee, Carly sat on the modern, overstuffed sofa in her new living room. She hadn't expected to find Alaska so beautiful. The subtle elegance, the immensity had enthralled her. Barren and dingy was what she'd been told to expect. Instead, she found the air crisp and clean. The skies were as blue as the Caribbean Sea. This state was so vast it was like a mother with her arms opened wide to lovingly bring the lost into her wide embrace.

"A mother . . ." Carly smiled absently. The perfect Freudian slip.

* * *

The nightmare returned that night. For years she'd been free of the terror that gripped her in the dark void of sleep, but that night she woke in a cold sweat, sitting up in bed and trembling. Perspiration dotted her face and she took several deep, calming breaths. The dream was so vivid. So real. What had brought back the childhood nightmare? Why now, after all these years?

As she laid her head against the pillow and closed her eyes, Carly attempted to form a mental image of her mother. Nothing came but a stilted picture of the tall, dark-haired stranger in the photo Carly had carried with her from foster home to foster home.

She woke the following morning feeling as if she hadn't slept all night. After the nightmare her sleep had been fitful, intermittent. Dark images played on the edges of her consciousness, shadows leaping out at her, wanting to engulf her in their dusk. Half of her yearned to surrender to the black void that beckoned, while the other half feared what she would discover if she ventured inside.

Brand St. Clair was sitting on the corner of her desk, one foot dangling over the edge, when Carly walked into the office later that morning.

"Morning." His greeting was casual.

"Hi." Carly's response was equally carefree. "Come to borrow another truck?"

"No. I thought I'd bring you coffee and a Danish as a peace offering."

Her gaze found the white sack in the center of the desk. "That wasn't necessary."

He opened the sack and took out a foam cup, removing the plastic lid before handing it to her.

"Thanks."

Brand removed a second cup for himself. "I don't suppose you do any bookkeeping on the side?"

The question took her by surprise. "My dear Mr. St. Clair, I am a traffic supervisor, not an accountant." A thin thread of humorous sarcasm ran through her voice. "I haven't studied bookkeeping since high school."

Amusement flashed across his handsome features. "I'd be willing to pay you to take a look at my books. The whole accounting system is beyond me."

"You're serious, aren't you?"

His smile fanned the deeply grooved lines at his eyes. Carly studied him and speculated that the crow's-feet weren't from smiling.

"I couldn't mean it more."

Carly took the chair and crossed her long legs, hoping he'd notice her designer nylons with their tiny blue stars. "Unfortunately, I've only had a few courses in bookkeeping. I'd only make matters worse." *Dear heavens,* Carly mused, stifling a laugh. She was flirting. Blatantly flirting! She hadn't done anything so outrageous in years. Her first impression of Brand yesterday was accurate. He was a wolf, all right, and more sensual than any man she'd ever known. There was more to him than met the eye—and her overwhelming response proved that there was more to her than she'd realized.

Whistling, George sauntered into the office, carrying a steaming mug in one hand.

"Good morning," he greeted in a cheery singsong voice. He seemed surprised to see Brand. "Good to see you, St. Clair. How did everything go yesterday?"

The glance Brand threw to Carly was decidedly uncomfortable. "Fine." The lone word was clipped and impatient.

"I talked to Jones this morning," George continued. "He explained the situation. I would have hated your losing that commission for lack of a truck."

"Commission?" Carly's dark eyes sparked with anger. "Was that before or after you rescued the poor injured hiker off Denali?"

"Hiker?" George's gaze floated from one to the other.

"You wouldn't have given me the truck otherwise," Brand inserted, ignoring George.

"You're right, I wouldn't have."

"I got a message that you wanted to see me." Brand directed his attention to George.

"As a matter of fact, I did." George adopted a businesslike attitude. "Come into the warehouse. I want to talk to you about something." He turned toward Carly and grinned sheepishly. "I don't suppose you'd mind putting on a pot of coffee? We're both going to need it before this morning's over."

Carly opened and closed her mouth. Coffee making hadn't been listed in her job description, but she complied willingly, rather than argue.

The two men were deep in conversation as they headed toward the door. Brand stopped and turned to Carly. "Think about what I said," he murmured, and smiled. It was one of those bone-melting, earth-shattering smiles meant to disarm the most sophisticated of women. But the amazing part of it all was that he didn't seem to recognize the effect he had on her. The gesture should have disarmed her; instead, it only served to confuse her further.

She was busy at her desk when Brand returned alone a half hour later.

"I meant what I said about paying you for some bookkeeping."

"I'm sorry," she returned on a falsely cheerful note, "but I'm busy. There's an important rescue I'm performing in Denali Park this weekend."

Brand didn't look pleased.

To hide her smile, Carly pretended an inordinate interest in her work, making a show of shuffling papers around. "Was there anything else?"

Slowly, his gaze traveled over her face, hesitating on her slightly parted lips. When he didn't answer right away, Carly looked up. She had been angry at his deception, disliking the way he'd gone about borrowing the truck. But one searing look and she had to fight her way out of the whirlpooling effect he had on her senses.

"Think about it," he said in a slightly husky voice.

"There isn't anything to think about," she returned smoothly, her tone belying the erratic pounding of her heart. When he walked out the door Carly was shocked to discover that her fingers were trembling. "Get a hold on yourself, old girl," she chastised herself in a breathy murmur, half surprised, half angry at her reaction to this man. Brand St. Clair had an uncanny knack for forcing her to recognize her own sensuality. And Carly hated it.

As the week progressed, Carly couldn't decide if she was pleased or disconcerted when she didn't see Brand again. Her job was settling into a routine aside from a few minor clashes with George. He gladly surrendered the paperwork to her, preferring that she handle the collection and claims while he took care of the routing.

On Friday afternoon Brand strolled through the office door and beamed her a bright smile. "Hello again."

"Hello." Carly forced an answering smile. "George is out for the day."

"I know. It's you I wanted to see."

"Oh." She swallowed uncomfortably, disliking the way her heart reacted to the virile sight of him.

"I just stopped by to see if you'd be interested in going flying with me tomorrow."

Carly stared at him blankly, confronted with the choice of owning up to what she was feeling or ignoring this growing awareness. In all honesty, she'd prefer it if he walked out the door and left her alone.

"Why me?" She didn't mean to sound so sharp, but she wanted to know what had prompted him to seek her out. Had she been flashing him subliminal messages?

His eyes narrowed fractionally. "I want your company. Is that a crime?"

Carly hesitated. His challenge was open enough, and she found that the answer came just as easily. She wanted this. True, Brand possessed a dangerous quality that captivated as well as alarmed her. One flight with him could prove to be devastating. But she'd love to fly. "How long will we be gone?" Not that it mattered; she hadn't planned to do anything more than unpack boxes.

"Most of the day. We'll leave in the morning and be back in time for me to take you to dinner." His low voice, with its faint drawl, was enticing.

"What time do you want me to meet you?" she asked. Red lights were flashing all around her, but Carly chose to ignore their warning. Brand St. Clair was a challenge—and she'd never been able to resist that. In some ways it was a fault, and in others it was her greatest strength.

The next morning, as Carly dressed in jeans and a thick jacket, she wondered at the wisdom of her actions. Only when she was strapped into the seat of the Cessna 150, her adrenaline pumping at the roar of the engine, did she realize how badly she wanted this. She started to ask Brand about the panel full of gages when she was interrupted by the voice of the air traffic controller, who gave them clearance for takeoff.

Brand turned and gifted her with another of his earth-shattering smiles before taxiing onto the runway and pulling back on the throttle. Then, with an unbelievable burst of power, they were airborne. Her stomach lurched as the wheels left the safety of the ground—but with exhilaration, not alarm.

Looking out the window, Carly watched as the ground below took on an unreal quality. She had flown several times, but sitting in a commercial airliner was a different experience than floating in the sky in a small private plane.

"This is fantastic." She shouted to be heard above the roar of the engines. The skies were blue with only a few powder-puff clouds, the view below unobstructed. "Will we see Mount McKinley?"

"Not this trip. We're headed in the opposite direction."

Carly responded with a short nod. She was anxious to view North America's largest mountain. Mount Rainier, outside Seattle, and the Cascade range featured distinctive peaks, but from what she'd read about McKinley, the mountain was more blunt, less angular than anything she'd seen.

"It's so green," she shouted, and pointed to the dense forest below. When Carly had made up her mind to take this job, her first thought had been that she would be leaving the abundant beauty of Washington behind. "I'm really impressed," she said with a warm smile.

Brand's gaze slid to her mouth. "What would it take for *me* to impress you?"

Carly threw back her head and laughed, refusing to play his game. There wasn't much he could do that would impress her more than he had already.

Brand took her hand and squeezed it. "What did your family think about you moving north?"

Rarely did Carly reveal her circumstances. "They didn't say anything. I'm over twenty-one." The lie was a minor one. She'd never known her father, and only God knew the whereabouts of her mother. The longest Carly had ever stayed in one foster home was four years. With only herself to rely upon, she'd become strong in ways that others were weak. Carly didn't need anyone but herself.

"How long have you been flying?" She diverted the questions from herself.

"Since I was a kid. My dad owned an appliance business and traveled all over Oregon. I took my first flying lessons at sixteen, but by that time I had been in the air a thousand times."

"Are you from Portland?"

He answered with an abrupt nod.

"What made you come to Alaska?"

He didn't hesitate. "The money."

Carly remembered George saying something about heavy expenses. "Medical bills, right?"

Brand turned to study her. Carly met his steely gaze. "Yes," he answered without elaborating. Carly didn't question him further.

His attention returned to the sky and Carly watched as a proud, invisible mask came over his face, blocking her out. It confused her. She was unsure of Brand, but he didn't intimidate her. In some ways she sensed that they were alike. Each had buried hurts that were best forgotten. Sighing, she glanced away. His attitude shouldn't bother her.

They were both quiet for a long time. "What do you think of Alaska?" Brand asked her unexpectedly, as if he were attempting to lighten the oppressive mood that had settled over them.

"I love it," Carly responded freely. "Of course, I haven't survived an Alaskan winter yet, so I might answer your question differently a year from now."

"A lot of people see Alaska as big and lonely. It's appeal isn't for everyone." His smile was wry.

"Alaska is isolated, that much I'll grant you. But not lonely. I've sat in a crowded room and been more alone than at any time in my life. Alaska demands and challenges, but not everyone is meant to face that."

Abruptly, Carly broke off and bit her lip. This was the very thing that had attracted her to this frozen land of America's last frontier.

Brand studied her, his expression revealing surprise at her answer. "George purposely hired someone in early spring," he told her. "Only a fool would move to Anchorage in winter."

"That bad?" She, too, hoped to lighten the mood.

"You have to live through one to believe it." The edges of his mouth deepened to reveal a smile.

"I'll make it," Carly returned confidently. She wasn't completely ignorant. Diana had taken delight in relaying the fact that temperatures of twenty degrees below zero weren't uncommon during the winter months in Anchorage. Carly had known what to expect when she'd accepted the job.

"I don't doubt that you will." His dark gaze skimmed her face. "I like you, Carly Grieves," he admitted, his voice low and gravelly, as if he hadn't meant to tell her as much.

"And I trust you about as far as I can throw you." A teasing light danced in her eyes. "But then, I'm stronger than I look."

They ate in a restaurant not far from the Anchorage airport. A companionable silence hung between them. The men Carly had dated in the past were talkers; she preferred it that way. The experience of sharing a meal with a man she had seen only a handful of times and feeling this kind of communication was beyond her experience. In ways she couldn't explain, it excited her.

They rode back to the airport, where Carly had left her car. "Come into my office and I'll show you around," Brand invited. "I'll put some coffee on."

"I'd like that."

He opened her car door for her, and she followed him into the small building that served as his office.

A flicker of uncertainty passed over Carly's features as she entered the one-room office. The area was too private, too isolated. Once inside the darkened room, Brand didn't make any pretense of getting coffee. Instead, he turned her into his arms, a hand on each shoulder burned through her thick jacket. He seared her with a bold look as his eyes ran over her face.

"I'm not interested in coffee," he muttered thickly.

"I knew that," she answered in a whisper.

His hand cupped the underside of her face as his thumb leisurely tested the fullness of her mouth. Slowly, his hand fell away and Carly involuntarily moistened her lips.

She watched, fascinated, as a veiled question flittered into his gaze. He looked as if he were making up his mind whether to kiss her or not. His fingers slid into her hair, weaving through the dark strands and tilting her head back. Although her heart was pounding wildly, she continued to study him with an unwavering look. His eyes were narrow and unreadable.

With a small groan, he fit his mouth to hers. Carly opened her lips in welcome. The kiss was the most unusual she had ever experienced: gentle, tender, soft . . . almost tentative. Gradually, he deepened the contact, his arms pulling her closer until she was molded tight against him. His hands roamed her back, arching her body as close as possible as his mouth courted hers, exploring one side of her lips and working his way to the other in a sensuous attack that melted any resistance.

He broke away, his mouth mere inches above hers. His warm breath fanned her face as his fingers worked the buttons of her coat. Again his mouth covered hers in long, drugging kisses as he slipped the coat from her shoulders and let it fall unheeded to the floor.

A hand slid under her blouse and cupped her breast, which swelled eagerly into his palm. His hips pinned her against the wall as his mouth demanded and took, giving as much as he was receiving.

Carly fought for control of her senses. This was too much, too soon, but she couldn't tear herself away. The throbbing ache his mouth, his hands, his body were creating within her was slowly consuming her will.

She moaned softly as he buried his face in the curve of her throat. Her eyes closed as she tangled her fingers in the hair that grew at the nape of his neck. Her taut breasts strained against the material of her blouse, craving the magic of his fingers.

"Brand." Breathlessly, she whispered his name, not sure why she had.

Instantly he went still, as if the sound of her voice had brought him to his senses. His hands closed painfully over her wrists and pulled them free.

"What's wrong?" she pleaded.

He dropped her hands and took a step in retreat. His eyes no longer met hers, but were cast down at the floor as he took in deep breaths. When he looked up and ran a hand along the back of his neck, Carly saw something flicker in his eyes. Regret? Guilt? Shock?

The world came to a forceful stop. She had been so stupid. A coldness settled over her as a painful hoarseness filled her throat.

"You're married, aren't you?"

Chapter Two

"No." Brand issued the single word with a vengeance.

"I'm not entirely stupid." Carly's voice became a tortured whisper.

"I'm a widower," Brand interrupted harshly, wiping a hand across his face.

It doesn't matter, Carly's mind screamed as she retrieved her coat. If she hadn't been so blinded by her pure physical attraction to him, she would have recognized those blatant red lights for what they were. His wife might be dead, but it didn't make any difference.

"Carly, listen."

She ignored him, damning herself for her own stupidity. "I had a great time today," she murmured with counterfeit enthusiasm.

"Carly, I want to explain."

She could hear the frustrated anger in his voice. The anger wasn't directed at her, but inward. Every dictate of her will was demanding that she turn around and run from the building. Both hands were tucked deep within her pockets as she took one step backward. "Thank you for dinner. We'll have to do it again sometime." Not waiting for his response, she turned and hurried from the office. By the time she reached her car, Carly's knees felt as though they could no longer support her.

When she arrived back at her apartment she thought she was going to be sick. *Brand had been married.* Forcing herself to breath evenly, she deliberately walked around the living room, running her hand over the back of the sofa. Everything she owned had been purchased new. She wouldn't take second best in anything. Not clothes, not cars, not jobs. After a life filled with secondhand goods and a hand-me-down childhood, she wasn't about to start now—especially with a man. All right, she was being unreasonable, she knew that; Diana had taken delight in telling her so a hundred times. But Carly didn't see any reason to change. She liked herself the way she was—unreasonable or not.

Three days later, she was still unable to shake the confusion and disappointment that Brand's announcement had produced. She'd made up her mind not to see him again under any conditions. Yet she discovered that her mind entertained thoughts of him at the oddest times. She forced his image from her brain, determined to blot him from her life completely.

Thursday evening, when the phone rang, Carly stared at it in surprise. The telephone company had installed it at the beginning of the week and, although she'd made several calls out, she had yet to receive one.

"Hello."

"Carly?" The voice reverberated, sounding as if it came from the moon.

"Diana? You idiot! What are you doing calling me? This must be costing you an arm and a leg." The soft echo of her words returned over the line.

"I couldn't stand it another minute. I had to find out how everything's going. I miss you like hell," Diana said softly. Then, as if she'd admitted more than she'd wanted, she quickly changed the subject. "How's Alaska? Have you seen any moose yet?"

"No moose and I love Alaska," Carly responded enthusiastically, knowing that her friend was uncomfortable sharing emotions. "It's vast, untouched, beautiful."

"That's not the way I heard it," Diana said and released a frustrated sigh. "How's the job and the mysterious George Hamlyn?"

"We've had a few minor clashes, but all in all everything's working out great."

"After all I did to convince you to stay in Seattle you wouldn't admit anything else," Diana chided. "How's the apartment?"

"Adequate. I'm looking into buying a condo."

"I knew it." Diana didn't bother to disguise her friendly censure. "I wondered how long you'd last in a *used* apartment."

"It's not that old," Carly responded with a dry smile. Her friend knew her too well.

"When are you going to get over this quirk of yours?"

"Quirk?" Carly feigned ignorance, not wanting to argue.

"No, it's become more than that." The teasing quality left Diana's voice. "It's an obsession."

"Just because I happen to prefer new things doesn't make me a candidate for the loony bin. I can afford the condominium." But barely. The payments would eat a huge hole into her monthly paycheck.

"How's Barney?" Carly quickly changed the subject. "Have you got a ring through his nose yet?"

Diana's laugh was falsely gay. "So-so. If I'm going to marry again, you can bet that this time I'm going to be sure."

"I've heard love is better the third time around."

"Love maybe, marriage never. Besides, that's supposed to be the *second* time around."

"In your case I had to improvise."

Diana gave a weak snort. "I don't know why I put up with you."

"I do," Carly supplied with the confidence of many years of friendship. "I'm the little girl you've always wanted to mother. Problem is, I'm only six years younger than you."

"I'm feeling every minute of thirty-one. Why'd you bring that up?"

"Good friend, I guess."

"Too good. Listen, sweetie, I'm worried about you. Don't let your damnable pride stand in the way if you want out of that godforsaken igloo."

"Honestly." Carly released an exasperated breath. "I'm perfectly capable of taking care of myself. So straighten up, crack the whip over Barney's head and quit being such a worrier. I'm doing fine on my own."

"True. You don't need me to louse up your life, especially since I've done such a bang-up job of screwing up my own. You'll write, won't you?"

"A letter's already in the mail," Carly assured her.

"I suppose I should hang up. This is probably costing me twenty bucks a minute."

"But I'm worth it."

Diana didn't hesitate. "You're the best friend I've ever had. Take care of yourself and let me know when you've come to your senses and want to head home."

"I will," Carly promised. But she wouldn't be moving back to Seattle. In fact, she doubted that she ever would. Alaska was too *right*. In a few short weeks it felt more like she thought a home should than anything she'd known as a child.

Late Friday afternoon, as Carly was working on a claim, George sauntered into the office, an oily pink rag dangling from his hip pocket. He'd been working with a mechanic. It hadn't taken Carly long to discover that George was a man of many talents.

"Get Brand St. Clair on the line for me," he said on his way to the coffeepot.

Carly's fingers tightened around the pencil she was holding. As much as she'd fought against it, Brand had remained on her mind all week.

Flipping through the pages of the telephone directory, Carly located Brand's number and punched the buttons of the phone with the tip of her eraser. She would be polite but distant, she decided. He hadn't made any attempt to contact her this week, so apparently he was aware of her feelings towards him.

With the receiver cradled against her shoulder, Carly continued working on her column of figures.

"No answer," she told her employer, hoping that relief in her voice was well disguised.

"Try again," George returned irritably. "That boy needs an answering machine. Lord knows he wears too many hats. He's working himself to death."

Carly had punched out Brand's number so many times by the end of the afternoon that she could have done it in her sleep. At five-thirty she straightened the top of her desk and removed her purse from the bottom drawer. George was talking to a mechanic when she stepped outside to tell him she hadn't been able to reach Brand.

"I never did get hold of St. Clair." The brisk wind whipped her shoulder-length hair about her oval face and stung her ivory complexion.

George glanced at Carly with a smile of chagrin. "Since it isn't out of your way, would you mind stopping off at his office and leaving a message on the door?"

Carly swallowed tightly. "Sure."

"Tell him I've got a couple of jobs for him next week and ask him to give me a call."

"Consider it done." She turned before he could see her mouth slant with displeasure. Not that she objected to doing George a favor. What she wanted was to avoid Brand. If someone were to see her and tell him she'd been by, he could misinterpret her coming.

The portion of the airfield that housed Brand's office was only a mile or so from Alaska Freight Forwarding. As Carly eased her blue Dodge into the space nearest his office, she noticed him walking toward her from the field. He'd obviously returned from a flight and had just finished securing his aircraft. Carly groaned inwardly and climbed out of her car.

Six days had passed since she'd last seen him, but time had done little to wipe out the pure physical impact of seeing him again. His glance was dry, emotionless, as he moved closer, his face lean and weathered from the sun. Mature.

"Hello." He stopped in front of her, revealing none of his feelings. The least he could do was look pleased to see her!

"George sent me over with a message." It was important that he understand she hadn't come of her own accord.

His nod was curt.

"He wanted me to tell you he has work for you next week if you're interested." She prayed the slight breathlessness in her voice would go undetected.

"I'm interested."

A shiver skipped over her skin at the lazy, sensual way he was studying her. Carly had the crazy sensation that his interest wasn't in the flying job.

"You're on your way home?" he asked her unexpectedly.

Her eyes refused to meet his. "Yes. It's been a long week." Damn. She shouldn't have said that. He might think she'd been sitting around by the phone waiting for him to call.

"Have you got time to stop someplace for a drink?"

"No." The word slipped out with the rising swell of panic that threatened to engulf her.

"Why not?" he demanded starky.

"Let's just say that I consider married men off limits. Even widowers. Especially widowers who have eyes that say, 'I loved my wife.' "

"I can't argue with you about that," Brand agreed easily. "I did love Sandra."

"That's the way it's suppose to be." Carly meant that. She couldn't imagine Brand not having loved...Sandra. Her mind had difficulty forming the name. It was easier to think of Brand's wife as a nonentity. The sudden urge for a cigarette was almost overwhelming. "Well, it was nice seeing you again." She fumbled in her purse for a Marlboro.

"Do you have anything against friendship?" Brand's features suggested a wealth of pride and strength. In the shadows of early afternoon, they appeared more pronounced.

"Everyone needs somebody." Reluctantly, she turned her eyes to his. She was thinking about Diana, the only true friend she'd ever had, as she lit the cigarette and inhaled deeply.

"Are we capable of that, Carly?" He refused to release her gaze.

Unable to find the words to answer him, she shrugged.

"Surely a drink between friends wouldn't be so bad."

She remained unsure. "I won't date you, Brand." Making that much clear was important.

"Not to worry." He beamed her a dazzling smile. "This isn't a date. Friends?" He extended his hand to her.

Her mind was yelling at her, telling Carly this whole idea was crazy. But it didn't seem to matter as she held out her hand to him for a curt shake.

Mentally chastising herself every block of the way, she followed him to a cocktail lounge, parking her car in the space beside his. Together they stepped into the dimly lit room. A girl at a piano on the far side of the open area was singing a low, sultry ballad.

Brand cupped her elbow, but when Carly involuntarily stiffened, he dropped his hand. "Sorry, I forgot we're just friends," he whispered as they walked across the room.

No sooner were they seated when a waitress appeared. Carly was undecided about what she wanted to drink, and while she was making up her mind, Brand took charge and ordered for her.

"I prefer to order for myself," she said after the waitress had gone, disliking the way he had taken control. She wasn't his date. Carly hated to be so petty, but protecting her heart was a necessity.

He went still, then shrugged. "Sorry, I keep forgetting."

He was strangely quiet then, Carly thought, considering the way he'd pressed the invitation on her. After a few minutes of small talk he settled back in his chair, seemingly content to listen to the piano singer.

"I don't know what to make of you." Carly spoke at last, uncomfortable with the finely strung tension between them.

"Little wonder," he said with a wry grin, and took a sip of his Scotch. "You've been on my mind all week."

Carly sat upright and leaned forward. "I don't think friends are necessarily on one another's minds."

He discounted her assessment with an ardent shake of his head. "Some friends are. Trust me here."

"The last man who asked me to trust him trapped me thirty thousand feet in the air and demanded that we make love."

"What did you do?" He straightened slightly, the line of his jaw tightening.

Carly smiled, taking a sip of her Tom Collins before she spoke. "Simple. I jumped. He was my skydiving instructor."

"Did everything turn out all right?"

"Depends on how you look at it. I wrenched my ankle and landed a mile off target. But on the other hand, it felt good to outsmart that creep."

"Lord, you live an adventuresome life."

"That's nothing compared to what happened to me the weekend I climbed Mount Rainier."

"I don't think I want to hear this," he murmured, nursing his drink. "Have you always had this penchant for danger?"

"It never starts out that way, but I seem to walk blindly into it." She leaned against the back of the chair, a hand circling her drink. The icy cold extended halfway up her arm.

"Have dinner with me?" A mock frown brought his brows together. "As friends, of course."

Carly knew she should tell him no, but something within her wouldn't let her refuse him. "All right, but I have the feeling I was safer on Mount Rainier."

He smiled as he rose and led the way into the restaurant that was connected to the lounge.

Once they were seated at the red, upholstered booth, a middle-aged waitress in a black skirt and peasant blouse handed them each a menu.

Quickly, Carly surveyed the items listed, mainly a variety of seafood and steak dishes. "If you don't mind, I'll order for myself this time," she teased, keeping her gaze centered on the oblong menu.

"Tom Collins was Sandra's favorite drink." Brand's low statement seemed to come out of nowhere.

"Oh, Lord," Carly shut her eyes tightly and set the menu aside. "I wish you hadn't told me that."

''I was just as shocked as you when it slipped out.''

Carly half slid from the booth. ''I think I'd better leave.''

''Don't go. Please.''

Carly had the impression he didn't often ask something of anyone. She stopped, her heart beating at double time.

''Did I ever tell you about the time I came face-to-face with a kodiak?'' he asked.

''A bear?''

His gaze was intent as he studied his water glass. ''Crazy as it sounds, I'm more frightened now.''

Carly plowed through her purse for another cigarette. ''Good grief, we're a fine couple.''

A smile slanted one side of his sensual mouth. ''We're only...''

''Friends.'' They said it together and laughed.

''All right,'' Brand said, and breathed in uncertainly. ''I'll admit it. This is the first time I've been out with a woman since Sandra died. She's been gone almost two years now. But the past is meant to be a guidepost, not a hitching post. I need a...friend.''

Carly ground out her half-smoked cigarette. ''Brand, I don't know.''

''You're not even trying. At least hear me out. It's been a while since I was into the dating scene. I realize you don't want to date me. I don't understand why, but that's up to you. But I was thinking that maybe I could practice with you. We could go out a couple of times until I see what kind of action there is.'' His tone was suddenly light, casual.

"Not on dates." Her fingers surrounded her own water glass and again the cold moved up her arm and stopped at her heart.

"No, these wouldn't be *real* dates."

"Just practice, until you find someone who interests you?" Her fingers tightened around the water glass as her tension mounted. Something deep inside her said she was going to regret this. Diana should be the one he was talking to. Diana was the rescuer. Not her.

Brand lifted his gaze until their eyes met, granting Carly the opportunity to study his face. His mood had shifted again, and now she realized that the look she had recognized earlier wasn't maturity, but pain. He'd been through hell. His wife's death had brought him to his knees and nearly broken him. Carly's senses leaped with a desire to ease that pain. She didn't often experience such intense feelings.

"I can't see how it would hurt, as long as we both understand one another," she said cautiously.

The waitress came and took their order.

"How'd we get so serious?" Brand's smile was forced, but the effort relaxed the rugged planes of his face and again Carly found herself responding involuntarily.

"I don't know."

"Let's talk about something else. As I recall, women like to talk about themselves."

"Not this woman. I'd bore you to death," Carly returned with a weak laugh. "I was born, grew up, graduated, found a job..." She hesitated, her eyes smiling into his. "Shall I continue?"

"Seattle?"

"Mostly." The tip of her index finger circled the rim of her glass. "What about you?"

He answered her question with another of his own. "What about men?"

"What about them?" Carly shot back.

"You've never married?"

"No." Her laugh was light. "Not even close."

"Sandra and I were barely out of college..."

Carly sighed with relief when the waitress returned, delivering their meals. She didn't want to hear about Brand's wife. Yet in another way it was good that she did, because it forcefully reminded her that she couldn't fall in love with Brand.

Carly's salad was piled high with crab. Lemon wedges dipped in paprika decorated the edges and thin slices of hard-boiled eggs defined the bowl. "This looks wonderful." Picking up her fork, she dipped into the crisp lettuce leaves. Brand followed suit, and they ate in silence. Several times during the meal Carly felt Brand watching her, his gaze disconcerting, making her uncomfortable.

"Did I commit some faux pas?" she asked, setting aside her fork as she met his eyes.

"No. Why?" Brand glanced up curiously.

"The looks you've been giving me make me think I've got Thousand Island dressing all over my chin."

"No, you haven't." Brand's chuckle was low and sensuous.

To avoid his look, Carly glanced into the lounge. Couples with arms wrapped around each other were dancing on the small polished floor to the slow music. Dancing had never been her forte, but the thought of Brand holding her produced a willful fascination. She shook her head to dispel the image.

"Do you dance?" she asked almost involuntarily. She didn't really want to know.

His fork paused midway to his mouth as he gave her a startled glance.

Hiding her uneasiness, Carly looked away. "Don't look so shocked. My interest was purely academic. It wouldn't be a good idea for us to dance."

"Why not?"

"Because—" She swallowed. Damn him. He was enjoying her discomfort. "Well, because of the close body contact . . . I just don't think it would be a good idea."

"But I'll need to practice a few times, don't you think?"

"No," she said, more forcefully than she had intended. "Dancing is like riding a bicycle. It all comes back to you even if you haven't gone riding in a long time." She pushed her plate aside, indicating that she was finished with her meal.

Brand didn't look up from his plate as he mumbled something under his breath. Carly didn't catch all of it, but what she did hear caused hot color to warm her cheeks. He'd said something about hoping that the same was true of sex.

While Brand paid for their dinner, Carly wandered outside. With hands thrust deep into her jacket pockets, she stared at the dark sky. The stars looked like rare jewels laid out on folds of black satin. The moonlight cleared a path through the still night. With her face turned toward the heavens, Carly walked past their parked cars and down the narrow sidewalk. Alaska was supposed to be cold and ruthless. Yet she felt warm and content, as if she belonged here and would never want to leave. Brand had reminded her that she hadn't suffered through an Alaskan winter. But the thought didn't frighten her. She was ready for that challenge.

Brand joined her. "Lend me one of those cigarettes," he said as he came up beside her.

"I didn't know you smoked." She watched as he lit up and exhaled a thin stream of smoke.

"Only rarely."

"Do I do this to you?"

"No," he said softly. "I want to tell you about Sandra, and having one of these gives me something to do with my hands."

Carly reached inside her purse and handed him the whole pack. She didn't want to hear about Sandra, but she recognized that Brand needed to tell her. If he talked things out with her, a virtual stranger, maybe then he could bury the past.

"We met in college. I guess I told you that, didn't I?"

Carly's hands formed fists deep inside her pockets. "Yes . . . yes, you did."

"She was probably one of the most beautiful women I've ever seen. Blonde and petite. And so full of life. You couldn't walk in a room full of people and not find Sandra. Funny thing, though—she was the quiet sort. She didn't like a lot of attention." The angles and planes of his face seemed to sharpen. "We were married almost eight years."

Carly's heart was pounding frantically. Each pain-filled word seemed to come at her like an assault. He didn't need to say how difficult it was for him to speak of his wife. It was evident in his voice, in the way he looked straight ahead, in the way he walked.

"She had myelocytic leukemia. The most difficult type to treat and cure. We knew in the beginning her chances of beating it were only one in five. Watching her die was agony." He paused, stamped out his cigarette butt, and lit another. "But death was her victory."

They continued walking for a long time, neither speaking. Carly didn't know what to say. Any words of comfort wouldn't have made it past the huge lump that had formed in her throat.

"I loved her," he said in a low, tortured voice. "A part of me will go to the grave grieving for Sandra."

Carly's heart swelled with emotion as she searched desperately for some way to communicate her regret. But no words would come. She wanted to tell him she understood how hard it must have been to release to death the one he loved. But she couldn't pretend to know how much it had cost him to watch his wife die.

Gently, she laid her hand on his forearm, wanting to let him know her feelings.

Brand's fingers gripped hers as he paused and turned toward her. Tenderly, he brushed the hair from her face and kissed her forehead. "Thank you," he said simply.

"I didn't do anything." Her voice sounded weak and wobbly even to her own ears.

"Just by listening you've done more than you know," he whispered and took her hand in his. Silently, their hands linked, they strolled down the moonlit sidewalk.

Carly had a difficult time sleeping that night. Brand hadn't attempted to hold or kiss her, and for that she was grateful. She didn't know if she had the strength to refuse him anything. The thought was scary. Everything about Brand confused and frightened her. If she had a rational head on her shoulders she wouldn't have anything more to do with him. But he was a rare kind of man, more rare than the gold that had prompted so many into Alaska's fertile land a hundred years before. She lay awake watching shadows dancing on the walls, taunting her. She shouldn't see him again, she told herself. Yet she could hardly wait for tomorrow afternoon, when they had planned to meet again.

Carly awoke the next morning with renewed determination. Brand needed her...for now. She didn't walk away from anything. Her independence, her

ability to meet challenges had become her trademark.
Friends didn't desert one another in times of need.
And this was a crucial time in Brand's life. A time of
transition. She would help him through that, be his
friend. Perhaps she would even have the opportunity
to introduce him to a few women.

Falling back against her pillow, Carly released a
long, tortured sigh. Who did she think she was kidding? Introduce Brand to another woman? She nearly
laughed out loud.

The phone rang just as she stepped into the shower.
Wrapping a towel around herself, she hobbled into the
living room, leaving a trail of water behind her.

"Yes," she breathed irritably into the receiver.

"Carly?" It was Brand. "You sound angry. What's
wrong?"

"Some idiot called and got me out of the shower."

"Don't tell me you're standing there naked." His
voice became low and slightly husky.

"I am standing in a puddle of water, catching a
chill."

His warm chuckle quickened her heartbeat. "I
won't keep you. I just wanted you to make sure you
hadn't changed your mind about this afternoon."

"I probably should. But no, I'll be ready when you
get here."

Carly dressed in designer jeans, cowboy boots and
a Western-style plaid shirt. She was putting the fin-
ishing touches on her makeup when the doorbell rang.
A hurried glance in the mirror assured her that she
looked fine.

"Good afternoon," she said, and smiled a greeting. Her heart warmed at the virile sight Brand presented in gray cords and a loose-fitting blue V-necked sweater. The long sleeves were pushed up past his elbows.

"I'm not dressed too casually, am I?" They were attending an art show. Diana thought Carly's generally informal dress outrageous. But Carly was herself and wore what she wanted, where she wanted. Cowboy boots and jeans sounded fine for an art show to her.

"Not at all." His eyes smiled boldly into hers. He wrinkled his nose appreciatively and sniffed the air. "What smells so good?"

"Probably my perfume," she said, and playfully exposed her neck to him.

"It smells like clams."

Carly released a heavy sigh. "I hope you realize that you're going to have to learn to be a little more romantic than that. I had a bowl of clam chowder for lunch."

"I'll try," he promised as he helped her into her three-quarter-length leather jacket.

"Tell me about the art show. I'm not much into the abstract stuff, but I like the Impressionists."

His hand snaked out across one shoulder. "You'll like this," He promised. "I don't want to tell you too much. I want your opinion to be unbiased."

"I know what I like."

"Spoken like a true expert."

The Anchorage Civic Center was crowded when they arrived, and they were forced to park down the street. Inside, people were clustered around a variety of paintings and sculptures.

With Brand at her side, Carly wandered from one exhibit to another. Not until she was halfway through the show did she see the painting of the child. Abruptly, she stopped, causing Brand to bump against her. He murmured something, but she didn't hear him as she walked to the lifelike oil painting.

The child was no more than five. Vulnerable, lost, hurting. Her pale pink dress was torn, the hem unraveled. Her scuffed shoes had holes, and one foot was dejectedly turned inward. The tousled hair needed to be combed. But it was the eyes that captured Carly's attention. Round, blue and proud. So proud they defied her circumstances. Carly stared at the painting for a long time before she noted that, in the far corner of one of the child's eyes, a tear had formed. Emotion rose within her. This was Carly as a child; this was the little girl in the nightmare.

Chapter Three

The dream ran through her mind like flickering scenes from a silent movie. She was small, not more than five, and hungry. So hungry that her stomach was empty and hurting. It was morning and she couldn't wake her mother. Several times she'd gone into the other bedroom and pulled at her mother's arm, but to no avail. At first Carly crawled back into her bed and cried, whimpering until she fell asleep. When she woke a second time, her stomach rumbled and gnawed at her. Sitting up, she decided she would cook her own breakfast.

The refrigerator was almost empty, but she found an egg. Mother always cooked those, and Carly thought she knew how. Filling the pan with water, she placed it on the stove and turned the knob. Then, afraid of a spanking, she ran into her mother's room and tried to shake her awake. But the dark-haired woman growled angrily at Carly and said to leave her alone.

Standing on a kitchen chair, Carly watched the egg tumble in the angry, boiling water. She didn't know how long Mama cooked things. Her mistake came when she pulled the pan from the stove. The bubbling water sloshed over the side and burned her small fingers. When she cried out and jerked her hand away, the pan of boiling water slid to the edge of the stove and toppled down her front.

This was the point where Carly always woke, usually in a cold sweat, her body rigid with terror. The dream had always been so vivid, so real. She didn't know if she had been burned as a child. No scars marred her body. There was only the dream that returned to haunt her at the oddest times.

"Carly." Brand's large hand rested on her shoulder. "Are you all right? You've gone pale."

"I want to buy this picture."

"Buy it?" Brand repeated. "It could run in the hundreds."

Carly shook her head and shrugged his hand from her shoulder. She didn't want him near. Not now. She raised her fingertips to her forehead and ran them down the side of her face as she continued to study the portrait. Of course, the child wasn't really her; she recognized that. The eyes were the wrong color, the hair too straight and dark. But the pain that showed so clearly through those intense eyes was as close to Carly's own as she had ever seen.

"The program states that this painting isn't for sale." Brand spoke from behind her.

Frustration washed through Carly. "I'll talk to the artist and change his mind."

"Her," Brand corrected softly. "Carly?" His voice contained an uncharacteristic appeal. "Look at your program."

Forcefully, she moved her gaze from the painting that had mesmerized her and glanced down at the sheet she'd been handed as she walked in to the center door. For a moment her gaze refused to focus on the printed description. The painting was titled simply "Girl. A Self-Portrait" by Jutta Hoverson.

"Is she here?" Carly was surprised at how weak her voice was. "I'd like to meet her."

Brand placed his hand on her shoulder, as if to protect her from any unpleasantness, a gesture Carly found almost amusing. "I think you should read the front of your program," he said gently.

He was so insistent that Carly turned it over to examine what it was Brand found so important. The instant she read the heading she sighed and sadly shook her head. The art show was a collection of works done by prisoners: murderers, thieves, rapists, and only God knew what else.

Carly lifted her gaze from the program to the oil painting. "I wonder what crime she committed."

"I thought you knew."

"It doesn't matter. I still want this picture," she murmured, noting the way Brand was studying her. She didn't want to explain why this was so important to her. She wouldn't.

"You feel more than just art appreciation," he said as his gaze skimmed her face thoroughly.

"Yes, I do." Levelly, she met his look, which seemed to pierce her protective shield. She opened her mouth to explain, but nothing came out. "I . . . I was poor as a child." She couldn't say it. Something deep and dark was restraining the words. Being raised in foster homes wasn't a terrible tragedy. She'd been properly cared for without the stigma that often accompanied girls in her circumstances. Having never known her mother might have been the best thing. The woman was a stranger, an alcoholic. For reasons of her own, her mother had never put Carly up for adoption. Carly resented that; the right to a normal family life had been denied her because her mother had refused to sign the relinquishment papers. As an adult, Carly thought that it wasn't love that had prompted her mother to hold on to her rights, but guilt.

"You might write"—Brand hesitated as he turned the program over, seeking the artist's name—"Jutta Hoverson and ask her to change her mind. It says here that she's at the Women's Correctional Center in Purdy, Washington. If I remember correctly, that's somewhere near Tacoma."

"I will," Carly confirmed. Jutta Hoverson might be a stranger, but already Carly felt a certain kinship with her. She continued to stare at the painting, having trouble taking her eyes from something that so clearly represented a part of her past. "There, but for the grace of God, go I." She hadn't meant to speak the words aloud.

"What makes you say that?" Brand questioned.

Carly's momentary glance of surprise gave way to a dry smile. "Several things." She didn't elaborate.

Although they spent another hour at the show, Carly's gaze continued to drift back to the painting of the child. Each time she examined it she saw more of herself: it was all there, in the dejected stance, the way one small foot was turned inward . . . in the hurt so clearly revealed in the eyes, the solitary tear that spoke of so much pain. So often in her life Carly had resisted crying, holding herself back until her stomach ached with the need to vent her emotion. Tears were considered a sign of weakness, and she wouldn't grant herself permission for such a display of helplessness.

The apartment looked bleak and dingy when they returned. Carly paused just inside the door, unable to decide if it was the apartment itself or her mood. Brand had followed her inside, although she hadn't issued an invitation.

"Carly." Just the way Brand said her name caused a warmth to spread through her. One large hand rested on each of her shoulders from behind. "Won't you tell me what's troubling you? You've been pensive and brooding all afternoon. Ever since you saw the painting."

"It's nothing," she said as she unzipped the leather jacket, forcing his hands from her shoulders as she slipped it from her arms and hung it in the closet. She couldn't very well ask him to leave without being rude, but she wanted to be alone for now.

"I'm sorry the show brought back memories you'd rather forget. But I think this is just the kind of thing friends are for. I spilled my guts last night. Now it's your turn." He lowered his long frame onto her sofa and leaned forward, his elbows resting on his knees, lacing his fingers together. "Talk. I'll try and be as good a listener as you were last night."

"I . . ." Carly's arms folded around her middle. "I . . . can't." She bit her lip. Brand's frustration was in his eyes for her to read. Her own feelings were ambivalent. She wanted to be alone, yet in an inexplicable way she wanted him there. The intense longing she felt for him to hold her was almost frightening. "What I need is time. Alone, if you don't mind."

"No problem." He jerked himself to his feet and was gone before she could say another word.

"Damn." She was being stupid and she knew it. But that didn't change the intensity of her feelings. Nor did it alter her black mood.

That night, Carly sat in the kitchen as she wrote a letter to Jutta Hoverson. Page after page of discarded attempts littered the table. There were so many things she wanted to say and no way she knew of putting them into words. After midnight, she settled on a few short sentences that simply asked Jutta if she would be willing to reconsider and sell the portrait.

Even after the letter was completed, Carly couldn't sleep. She hadn't meant to offend Brand, but she clearly had. He had revealed a deep and painful part of his own past, and she had shunned him this afternoon when it would have been natural to tell him why the painting had made such an impression on her.

She'd hesitated to open herself to him. The words had danced in her mind, but she'd been unable to say them. True, she didn't make a point of telling people her circumstances, but she didn't hide them either. Something about the afternoon—and Brand—had made her reluctant to reveal her past.

No more sure of the answers when she awoke the next morning, Carly dressed and put on a pot of coffee. On impulse, she decided to phone Diana. Sometimes her friend could understand Carly better than she did herself. After ten long rings, she replaced the receiver. Diana had probably spent the night with Barney. She wished those two would marry. As far as Carly could tell, they were perfect for one another. Barney was the first man Diana had ever loved who didn't need to be rescued from himself. Invariably, Diana fell for the world's losers; she apparently felt her undying love would redeem them. After two disastrous marriages, Diana was in no hurry to rush to the altar a third time. But Barney was different. Surely Diana could see that. He loved Diana. Barney might not be Burt Reynolds, but he was wonderful to Diana, and Carly's friend deserved the best.

Carly spent the morning writing Diana a long letter, telling her about the painting and Jutta Hoverson. Almost as an afterthought, she decided to add a few lines about Brand and their...*friendship*. She'd only meant to say a few things, but writing about her reactions to him helped her to understand what was happening. A couple of lines quickly became two long pages.

Both letters went in Monday's mail.

By Wednesday, Carly still hadn't heard from Brand. Apparently, he'd come into the office one afternoon while she was out, but had spoken with George and hadn't left a message for her. That evening, Carly decided she couldn't bear another night of television. Shopping was sure to cure even the heaviest of moods.

Before Carly knew where she was headed, she found herself on the sidewalk outside of Brand's apartment house. After punching out his phone number so many times that past Friday, Brand's address had become embedded in her memory. His late-model car was parked against the curb. She didn't know which apartment was his, but all she'd need to do was look at the mailboxes.

Her first knock was tentative. Coming to see him was a *friendly* gesture, she assured herself. And she did feel bad about the way she'd behaved Saturday.

"Yes?" The door was jerked open impatiently. Brand stopped abruptly as surprise worked its way across his handsome features. "Carly." He whispered her name.

"Hi." Cheerfully, she waved her hand. "I was in the neighborhood and thought I'd stop in and see how you were doing. But if this is a bad time, I can come back later."

"No, of course not. It's a great time. Come on in." He stepped aside and ran his hand along the back of his neck.

Carly had to smile at the stunned look on his face. As she stepped inside, she noted that the interior of the apartment was stark. Carpet, furniture, drapes—nothing held the stamp of Brand's personality or made this home distinctly his. Strangely, Carly understood this. Since Sandra's death Brand's life had been in limbo. He carried on because time had pushed him forcefully into doing so. She imagined that he didn't even realize how stark his home and his existence had become.

"Actually, your timing couldn't be better," he said as he led the way into the kitchen. The apartment wasn't as spacious as her own. The living room blended into the kitchen and the round table was covered with a variety of slips and paper. "I was trying to make heads or tails out of this bookkeeping nonsense. It might as well be Greek to me."

"I don't suppose you'd like some help?" Carly volunteered, and laughed at the relief that flooded his face.

"Are you crazy? Does a starving man reject food?" Turning one scratched oak chair around, Brand straddled it, looking somewhat chagrined. "I insist on paying you."

Mockingly, Carly pushed a ledger aside. "No way. Isn't helping each other out what friends are for?" His eyes smiled into hers, and she noted the lines that fanned from their corners in deep grooves. The realization that those lines weren't from laughter was reinforced as she caught sight of a framed picture on the television. *Sandra*. Carly's heart leaped into her throat.

Brand's gaze followed hers. "I told you she was beautiful."

Beautiful. The word exploded in her mind. Sandra had been far more than that. She was exquisite. Perfect. Carly scooted out of her chair and walked across the room, lifting the picture to examine it more closely. Blonde and petite, just as Brand had described. But vibrant. Her blue eyes sparkled with laughter and love. This woman had been cherished and adored, and it was evident in everything about her that she'd returned that love in full measure.

"She was an only child," Brand explained. "Her father died of a heart attack shortly after we learned that Sandra had leukemia. Her mother went a year after Sandra. I think grief killed her. She simply lost the will to live."

Carly couldn't do anything more than nod. She was gripping the picture frame so hard that her finger ached. She forced herself to relax, replacing the photograph on top of the television.

"There's another in the bedroom with Shawn and Sara, if you'd like to see that one."

Carly shook her head emphatically. The way she had reacted to that one picture was enough. Shawn and Sara? Did Brand have children? Certainly he would have explained if the two were his children. He would have mentioned them long before now. No, they were probably a nephew and niece. They had to be. Knowing that Brand had been married had been enough of a blow. Adding children to that would be her undoing.

Carly gave herself a vigorous mental shake. Brand could have ten children and it shouldn't bother her. She was his friend. They weren't dating. Saturday had been just another of their "this-is-not-a-date" outings. Even her coming to his place today hadn't been anything more than a friendly gesture.

Coming to stand beside her, Brand lifted the photo from the television. Carly heard him inhale deeply. "I think the time has come to put this away."

"No." The word came out sounding as if she'd attempted to swallow and speak at the same time. Carly wanted him to keep the picture out to serve as a reminder that she couldn't allow her feelings for him to shift beyond the friendship stage.

He ignored her protest, staring at the photo as if he were saying good-bye. A deep frown marred his brow. "I can't very well bring a woman to my apartment and have a picture of my wife sitting out," he explained reasonably.

Carly had difficulty swallowing. "I guess you're right."

He carried the picture into another room and returned a moment later. Carly was at the table, looking over the accounting books, pretending she knew what she was doing. Her bookkeeping classes had been years ago.

"Is what happened last weekend still bothering you?"

Carly shrugged her shoulders. "I suppose you've guessed that I had a troubled childhood." Her fingers rotated the pencil in nervous reaction, and she didn't meet his eyes; instead, she focused her gaze on the light green sheets of the ledger. "The state took me away from my mother when I was five. I don't remember much about her. I got a letter from her once when I was ten. She was drying out in an alcoholic treatment center and wrote to say that she'd be coming for me soon and that we'd be a real family again. She sent her picture. She wasn't very pretty." Carly paused, thinking that the family resemblance between them was strong. Carly wasn't pretty either. Not like Sandra.

"What happened?" Brand prompted.

Carly set the pencil on the table and interlaced her fingers. "Nothing. She never came."

"You must have been devastated." Brand resumed his position in the chair beside her, his voice gentle, almost tender.

"I suppose I was, but to be truthful, I don't remember. At age twelve I was sent to the Ruth School for Girls for a time, until another foster home could be found. That was where I met my friend, Diana. Since then we've been family to one another—the only family either of us needs." Her voice was slightly defensive.

"But who raised you?"

"A variety of people. Mostly good folks. With all the horror stories I've heard in recent years, I realize how fortunate I was in that respect."

"The art show upset you because you saw yourself in that portrait." His observation was half question, half statement.

"That picture was me at five. Seeing it was like looking at myself and reliving all that unhappiness."

Brand reached out and tenderly cupped the underside of her face. Carly's hands covered his as she closed her eyes and surrendered to the surging tide of emotion.

Brand didn't say a word. He didn't need to. His comfort was there in his healing touch as he caressed the delicate slope of her neck. His fingertips paused at the hammering pulse at the hollow of her throat before lightly tracing the proud lift of her chin.

"You're a rare woman, Carly Grieves," he whispered huskily.

Their eyes met and held. They were two rare souls. The wounded arctic wolf and the emotionally crippled little girl.

Slowly, ever so slowly, his hands roamed from the curve of her neck to her shoulders, cupping them and deliberately, tantalizingly, drawing her mouth to his.

Her lips trembled at the feather-light pressure as his mouth softly caressed hers. This wasn't a kiss of passion, but one of compassion.

Confused emotions assaulted her. She knew what he was trying to convey, but she didn't need or want his sympathy. Her hand curved around the side of his face, her fingers curling into the thick hair at his nape. "Brand," she whispered urgently, the moist tip of her tongue outlining his mouth.

He moaned as he hungrily increased the pressure, his arms half lifting her from the chair as he claimed her lips with a fierceness that stole her breath—and melted her resistance.

Simultaneously, they stood, their bodies straining against one another as their mouths clung. His tongue probed the hollow of her mouth, meeting hers in dancing movements that sent wave after wave of rapture cascading through her. His hands found her hips and buttocks as he molded her against his unyielding strength. Her senses exploded at the tantalizing scent of tobacco and musk and the taste of his tongue.

The profound need building within Carly was quickly becoming a physical ache. Her hard-won control vanished under the onslaught on his touch. Her cool, calm head—the one that before this had reacted appropriately to every situation—deserted her. Raw desire quivered through her, warming her heart and exposing her soul.

Breaking the contact, Brand's eyes locked with hers. He seemed to be searching for some answer. Carly could give him none, not understanding the question. Together, their breaths came ragged and sharp as they struggled to regain their composure. Carly fought desperately for her equilibrium and pressed her forehead against the broad expanse of his chest.

"Are friends supposed to kiss like that?" Her voice was barely above a whisper.

Brand's arms went around her as he rested his chin against the crown of her head. "Some friends do." He didn't sound any more in control of himself than she did.

"I'm...I'm not sure I'm ready for you to be this type of friend." A rush of cool air caressed her heated flesh, bringing her gradually back to reality. Gently, but firmly, she pulled free from his embrace. Suddenly she felt naked and confused. Kissing Brand was like striking the head of a match; their desire for one another overpowered common sense. They'd only known each other a short time and yet she was weak and without will after only a few kisses. Diana wouldn't believe she was capable of such overwhelming emotion. Carly had trouble believing it herself.

"I've frightened you, haven't I?"

Her arms were folded across her stomach. "Brand, I'm twenty-five years old. I know what to expect when a man kisses me." Carly knew she sounded angry, but that anger was directed more at herself than him.

His low laugh surprised her. "I'm glad *you* know about these things because I feel as shaky as I did the first time I kissed a woman. It's been over two years since I've made love."

Carly's hands flew to her ears. She didn't want to hear this. Not any of it. With brisk strides, she walked to the other side of the room. Coming here today had been a colossal mistake. One she wouldn't repeat— ever.

"Gee, look at the time." She glanced at her gold wristwatch and slapped her hands against her sides. "Time passes quickly when you're having fun, or so they say."

"Carly?" he ground out impatiently.

She took a couple of steps in retreat until she found herself backed against the front door. She turned, her hands locking around the doorknob in a death grip.

"I'll talk to you later in the week," Brand murmured, and just the way he said it told her that their next meeting wouldn't end with her running out of the door like a frightened rabbit.

The phone was ringing when Carly stepped through the door of her apartment. Thinking it might be Brand, she stared at it several long seconds while she shrugged off her jacket. No, he wouldn't phone. Not so soon.

"Hello," she answered, a guarded note in her voice.

"Carly, it's Diana."

"Diana!" Carly burst out happily. Rarely had there been a time she'd needed her friend more. "You can't afford these calls, but thank God you phoned."

"What's up? You sound terrible and it's not this crummy long-distance echo, either."

"It's a long story." It wasn't necessary to explain everything to Diana; just hearing her voice had a soothing effect. "Tell me what prompted this sudden urge to hear my voice."

"I couldn't stand it another minute." Diana laughed lightly. "Your letter arrived and I didn't want to have to write and wait for your reply. Tell me about him."

Carly's heart sank. "Do you mean Brand?"

"Is there someone else I don't know about?"

Stepping over the arm of her sofa, Carly walked across the couch, dragging the telephone line with her as she went. "There's nothing to tell. We're only friends."

"When you show this much enthusiasm for any male, I get excited. Now what's this bull about the two of you just being friends? Who are you kidding?"

"Diana . . ." She exhaled a trembling breath as she sat down. "I don't know what to think. Brand's been married."

"So? If you remember correctly, I've left two husbands in my wake."

"But this is different. She died of leukemia and it nearly killed him, he loved her so much."

"Well, sweetie, I hate to say it, but this guy sounds perfect for you. You're two of a kind. Both of you are walking through life wounded. Has he gotten you into bed yet?"

"Diana!" Carly was outraged. Hot color seeped slowly up her neck.

"I swear, you must be the only twenty-five-year-old virgin left in America."

"If you don't stop talking like that, I'm going to hang up," Carly threatened.

"All right, all right."

Carly could hear Diana's restrained laughter. The woman loved to say the most outrageous things just to get a rise out of Carly.

"Take my advice." Diana's tone was more serious now. "You can hunt all your life for the perfect male and never find him. He doesn't exist. And even if by some fluke of nature you find someone who suits you, he's liable to expect the perfect female. And neither one of us is going to fill those shoes."

Crossing her legs Indian-style beneath her, Carly managed a weak sigh. "I suppose you're right."

"I'm always right, you know that," Diana responded with a small laugh. "Now, listen, because I've got some serious-type news."

"What?" Carly straightened at the unusually deep intonation in Diana's voice.

"Against my better judgment and two miserable failures, Barney has convinced me that we should get married."

"Diana, that's wonderful. *You* two are the ones who belong together. This is fantastic."

"To be honest, I'm rather pleased about it myself. I'm not getting any younger, you know, and I'm ready to face the mommy scene. Barney and I've decided to have a family right away. Can you picture me pinning diapers and the whole bit?"

"Yes," Carly returned emphatically. "Yes, I can. You'll make a wonderful mother."

"Time will tell," Diana chuckled. "At least I know what *not* to do."

"We both do," Carly agreed. "Have you set the date?"

"Next month, on the fifteenth."

"But that's only a little over three weeks away."
Mentally, Carly was chastising Diana and Barney for
not getting their act together sooner. This was one
wedding she didn't want to miss. But she could hardly
ask for time off now.

"Believe me, I know. But the wedding won't be anything fancy. It'd be ridiculous for me to march down
the aisle at this point. Barney and I want you here. It's
important to both of us."

Disappointment made Carly's hand tighten around
the receiver. "I can't, Diana," she said with an exaggerated sigh. "Why couldn't you have made up your
mind before I left Seattle?"

"Barney insists on paying your airfare. Now, before you say a word, I know about that pride of yours.
But let me tell you from experience, it's better not to
argue with Barney and all his money. So plan right
now on being here."

Carly would have enjoyed nothing more. "But I
can't ask for time off from work. Hamlyn would have
my head."

"Threaten to quit," Diana returned smoothly. "If
Hamlyn gives you any guff, tell him where to get off.
By this time he's bound to recognize what a jewel you
are."

"Diana, I don't know."

Some of the teasing quality left Diana's voice.
"You're the closest thing I've got to family, Carly. I've
been married twice and both times I've stood before a
justice of the peace and mumbled a few words that

were as meaningless as the marriage. I want this time
to be right—all the way."

Carly understood what Diana was saying. She
hadn't been present at either of her friend's other
weddings. "I don't care what it takes," Carly replied
staunchly, "wild horses couldn't keep me away."

"Great. I'll let you know the details later. We're
seeing a minister tonight. Imagine me in a church!"
She laughed. "That should set a few tongues wag-
ging!"

"I'll phone sometime next week," Carly promised
as she replaced the receiver. A smile softened the tense
line of her mouth. Diana a mother! The mental picture of her friend burping a baby was comical enough
to lighten anyone's mood. But she'd be a good one. Of
that Carly had no doubt.

The days flew past. Carly dreaded seeing Brand, but
she didn't doubt that he'd be true to his word. The
next time they were together could prove to be uncomfortable for them both. He wouldn't avoid a confrontation, that she recognized.

Friday afternoon, George casually mentioned that
Brand was on a flying assignment and wouldn't be
back until the following day. Carly breathed easier at
the short reprieve. At least she would have more time
to think about what she wanted to say to him. One
thing was sure: it would be better if they didn't continue to see one another. Even for *non*-dates. She
didn't know what unseen forces were at work within
her, but Brandon St. Clair was far too appealing for
her to remain emotionally untouched. He needed a

woman. But not her. She'd make that clear when she saw him. Once it was stated, she could go back to living a normal, peaceful life. She might even investigate learning to knit. By the time Diana was pregnant, Carly might have the skill down pat enough to knit booties, or whatever it was babies wore.

Carly was sorting through her mail late Friday afternoon, still thinking about motherhood and how pleased she was for her friend. As she shuffled through several pieces of junk mail, when a handwritten envelope took her by surprise. Glancing at the return address, she noted it was from the Women's Correctional Center in Purdy. The name on the left-hand corner was Jutta Hoverson.

Chapter Four

Memories of the proud child in the oil painting ruled Carly's thoughts as she clutched Jutta Hoverson's reply. Bitter disappointment was washing through her. The letter had been direct and curt. Jutta Hoverson hadn't bothered with a salutation. I TOLD THE PEOPLE TO SAY THAT THE PAINTING IS NOT FOR SALE. I DON'T WANT TO SELL THIS ONE. Her large signature was scrawled across the bottom of the lined paper. And then, as if in afterthought, Jutta had added: I HAVE OTHER PAINTINGS. She'd provided no information. No prices. Not that it mattered; Carly only wanted the one.

She must have read Jutta's brusque words a dozen times, seeking a hidden meaning, desperately wanting to find some clue that the woman was willing to sell the self-portrait. There hadn't been many things in her life that Carly had wanted more than that painting. A week after the art show, the small child remained vivid in her memory; she could still envision the proud tilt of her chin and the hidden tear in the corner of one eye. So many times in her life Carly had joked about her past. If someone had questioned her about being raised as she was, Carly's flippant reply was always the same: Superman had foster parents. Even in the bleakest moments of her life, Carly had forced herself to be optimistic. Her childhood had made her emotionally strong and fortified her fearless personality. But tonight, with the letter from Jutta in her hand, Carly didn't feel like playing a Pollyanna game. She felt like eating twenty-seven chocolates, soaking in the bathtub, reading a book and downing an aspirin...all at the same time. A weak smile hovered at the corners of her tight lips. Diana would get a kick out of that.

As it turned out, Carly didn't do any of those things. She went to a theater and paid to see a movie she couldn't remember. She sat in the back row and slouched so far down that she had trouble seeing the screen. After devouring two bags of popcorn, she returned home and downed half a jar of green olives.

Carly woke the next morning depressed and slightly sick to her stomach. Her mood swings weren't usually so extreme. She liked to think of herself as an even-keeled sort of person, although Diana claimed she was eccentric. Admittedly, she didn't know anyone else who slept with knit socks on her feet or kept earmuffs on her nightstand in case of a storm so she wouldn't hear the thunder. What an ironic sort of person she was. Unafraid of change or danger, Carly often leaped into madcap schemes without thought.

She knew Diana had worried herself sick the weekend Carly had climbed Mount Rainier. The only mountain climbing she'd ever done had been that one weekend on Washington State's highest peak. And yet, Carly was frightened of a tempest.

A long walk that morning released some of her inner tension. Her fingers pressed deep within the side pockets of her tight jeans, she kicked at rocks and pieces of broken glass along the side of the road. Something green flittered up at her. The reflection of the lazy rays of the sun flashed on a discarded and broken wine bottle. Carly stooped to pick it up. It was a broken piece of glass, with its edges worn smooth by time. Feeling a little like a lost child, Carly tucked the fragment into her pocket. A rush of emotion raced through her. *She* was like that glass. Discarded and forgotten by her mother, scoured by time.

Carly had followed her feet with no clear destination in mind, and soon found herself in a park. The happy sound of children's laughter drifted toward her. She stood on the outskirts of the playground, watching. That was the problem with her life, she mused seriously. She was always on the outside looking in.

Well, not anymore, her mind cried. *Not anymore.* With a determination born of self-pity, she ran to the slowly whirling merry-go-round.

"Hi." A boy of about seven jumped off a swing and climbed onto the moving merry-go-round. "Are you going to push?"

"I might." Carly started to trot around. The boy looked at her as if she were a wizard who had magically appeared for his entertainment.

"Didn't your mother ever tell you not to talk to strangers?" Carly asked him as she ran, quickly losing her wind. She climbed onto the ride and took several deep breaths.

"You got kids?" the boy countered. "I think it would be all right if you had kids."

"Nope. There's only me." But Carly wasn't trying to discourage his company. She had no desire to be alone.

The boy's brows knit in concentration, then he gave Carly a friendly grin. "You're not a real stranger. I've seen you in the Safeway store."

Carly laughed and jumped off the merry-go-round to head toward the swing set.

"I saw you buy Captain Crunch cereal." He said it as if that put her in the same class as Santa Claus and the Tooth Fairy. He ambled to the swing set and took the one beside her, pumping his legs and aiming his toes for the distant sky until he swung dangerously high. Carly tried to match him, but couldn't.

"I saw you pick up something on the path. What was it?"

"An old piece of glass," Carly answered, still slightly out of breath.

"Then why'd you take it?" He was beginning to slow down.

"I'm not sure."

"Can I see it?"

"Sure." Using the heels of her shoes to stop the swing, she came to a halt and stood to dig the piece of glass from her pocket.

The young boy's eyes rounded eagerly as she placed it in the palm of his hand. "Wow. It's neat."

It was only a broken, worn piece of a discarded wine bottle to Carly. Tossed aside and forgotten, just as she had been by a mother she couldn't remember.

"See how the sun comes through?" He held it up to the sky, pinching one eye closed as he examined it in the sunlight. "It's as green as an emerald."

"Feel how smooth it is," Carly said, playing his game.

The boy rubbed it with the closed palms of his hands and nodded. "Warm like fire," he declared. "And mysterious, too." He handed it back to her. "Look at it in the light. There's all kinds of funny little lines hidden in it, like a treasure map."

Following his example, Carly took the green glass and held it up to the sun. Indeed, it was just as the young boy had said.

The muffled sound of an insistent voice came from the other side of the park.

"I gotta go," the boy said regretfully. "Thanks for letting me see your glass." Taking giant steps backward, he paused to glance apprehensively over his shoulder.

"Would you like to keep it?" Carly held it out for him to take.

His eyes grew round with instant approval, then darkened. "I can't. My mom will get mad if I bring home any more treasures."

"I understand," Carly said seriously. "Now, get going before you worry your mother." She waved to him as he turned and kicked up his short legs in a burst of energy.

Carly's hand closed around the time-scoured glass. It wasn't worthless, as she'd thought, but a magical, special piece. What else was there that was as green as an emerald, as warm as a fire and as intriguing as a treasure map? Tucking it back in her pocket, she strolled toward her apartment, content.

Stopping off at the supermarket, Carly returned home with a bag full of assorted groceries. The flick of a switch brought the stereo to life. The strains of Carole King's voice filled the small room with "You've Got a Friend." Carly hummed as she unloaded the sack. Unbidden, the image of Brand fluttered into the untamed edges of her mind. She straightened, her hand resting on the gentle curve of her hip. Brand was her friend. The only real friend she'd made in Anchorage.

The soft beat of the music continued, causing Carly to stop and ponder. The song said all she had to do was call his name and he'd be there, because he was her friend.

But Brand was flying today. At least, George had said he wouldn't be back until late afternoon.

Maybe she should phone him just to prove how wrong that premise was. Carly reached for her phone and punched out Brand's number. Her body swayed to the gentle rhythm of the song and she closed her eyes, lost in the melody.

"Hello," Brand answered gruffly.

The song faded abruptly. "Brand? I didn't think you'd be back." Her heart did a nonsensical flip-flop. "I...ah...how was your trip?" She brushed the bangs from her forehead, holding them back with her hand. The phone cord stretched into the kitchen and she leaned a hip against the counter.

"Tiring. How are you?"

"Fine," she answered lightly, disliking the way her pulse reacted to the mere sound of his voice. As much as she hated to admit it, Carly had missed Brand. Then, to fill an awkward pause: "The radio's playing 'You've Got A Friend.'"

"I can hear it in the background."

Carly could visualize Brand's faint smile.

"I heard from Jutta Hoverson." Her fingers tightened around the receiver.

"Jutta...oh, the artist. What did she say?"

Carly exhaled a pain-filled sigh. "She's not interested in selling."

"Carly, I'm sorry." Brand's voice had softened perceptibly. "I know how much you wanted that painting."

"I'll bet you're hungry," she surprised herself by saying. "Why don't you come over and I'll fix you something? Friends do that, you know."

"I'll be there in ten minutes."

Brand sounded as surprised by the invitation as she was at making it. But it *was* understandable, Carly mused; she wanted to be around people. If she'd been in Seattle, she'd have wandered around the waterfront or Seattle Center. Finding a touristy crowd in Anchorage was more difficult.

Setting up a tray of deli meats and a jar of olives, Carly realized that her mood required more than casual contact with the outside world. She wanted Brand. The comfort his presence offered would help eliminate the bitter edge of Jutta's refusal to sell the painting. Wanting Brand with her was a chilling sensation, one that caused Carly to bite her bottom lip. She didn't want Brand to become a habit, and being with him could easily become addictive.

The doorbell chimed. She glared at the offending portal, angry with herself for allowing Brand to become a weakness in her well-ordered life.

"Hi." She let him in, welcoming him with a faint smile.

"Here—I thought these might brighten your day." Brand handed her a small bouquet of pink and white carnations and sprigs of tiny white flowers. The bouquet wasn't the expensive florist variety, but the cheaper type from the supermarket.

Without a word, Carly accepted the carnations, her fingers closing over the light green paper that held them together. Brand's gesture made her uneasy. Flowers were something he would do for a *date*. And George had mentioned something about the heavy medical bills Brand was paying off. His *wife's* bills. A weary, disgruntled expression moved over her face.

"What's the matter?" Brand looked into her troubled eyes.

Carly lowered her chin, not wanting him to see how affected she was. "Nothing."

"Are we back to that?" Irritation marked his words. "Have we regressed so far in such a short time?"

"What do you mean?" She raised her head, barely managing to keep her voice calm and firm. Moistening her lips was an involuntary action that drew Brand's attention and confusion marred his features as he struggled with himself. He wanted to take her in his arms and hold her; it was written in his eyes. He knotted his hands, and Carly recognized anew the strength of the attraction that pulsed between them. The knowledge should have given her a feeling of power, but instead it angered her further.

"We went to the art show and it was obvious something was troubling you," Brand continued, his tone accusing. "I wanted you to tell me on your own. But you made me ask. I don't remember your exact words, but the message was clear. There was nothing wrong." His voice became heavy with sarcasm. "Well, damn it, Carly, there *was* something wrong then, just as there's something the matter now. I have a right to know."

Carly shaped her mouth into a hard line, her eyes snapping brown fire. The carnations all but burned her fingers as she tossed them carelessly on top of the counter and whirled around, her heart racing wildly.

"No," Brand barked impatiently. He inhaled a steadying breath. "No," he repeated and his hands settled to either side of her neck and pulled her toward him. "I won't let you do it, Carly. I'm not going to fight with you. Not when you've wiggled your way into my every waking thought for the past week."

Pride demanded that she shrug a shoulder in an effort to free herself. But Brand's hold tightened, his fingers forcing her so close to him that she could feel his warm breath. A raging battle warred in her thoughts. She damned herself for craving the comfort of his arms, and in the same breath, she reached for him. Not smiling. Not speaking.

Needing was something new to her, and Carly didn't like to admit to any weakness.

Brand's arms slipped around her waist and drew her into his embrace. The only sound in the room was the radio, playing a low and seductive melody from the far corner.

He didn't try to kiss her, although she was sure he wanted to. He knew she needed comfort at that moment, and restrained himself from putting his physical needs before her emotional ones. Carly was grateful for his restraint. Her defenses had been kicked low. His hand cupped the side of her face, pinning her ear against his heart. She could hear the uneven thud and realized that she was capable of doing the same things to him as he did to her. She knew they were bad for one another, but for now it felt so good to be comforted and secure. Good...bad... Confused,

Carly didn't know what to think anymore. All she knew was that she was too weak to fight. Not now.

"I thought you offered to feed me," Brand said after a long, drawn-out moment, his voice husky enough to betray her effect on him.

"Are sandwiches all right?" She turned and brought out the tray of deli meats and the bottle of green olives, setting them on the counter. A loaf of bread followed, along with a jar of mayonnaise and another of mustard.

"Fine. I could eat a ..." He paused as he surveyed the contents of the plate. " ... pastrami, turkey, beef and green olive sandwich any day."

"There are Twinkies for dessert."

"Good," Brand replied absently as he built a sandwich so thick Carly doubted that it would fit into his mouth.

After constructing her own, she joined Brand at the kitchen table. "I guess I should have warned you that my cooking skills are limited." She popped an olive into her mouth.

"Don't apologize."

"I'm not. I'm just explaining that you'll have to take me as I am. Fixing a meal that requires a fork is beyond my capabilities."

Chuckling, he lifted his napkin and dabbed a spot of mustard from the corner of his mouth. "Do you think there's any chance that Jutta will change her mind and sell the painting?"

The letter was on the table and Brand couldn't help but notice it. Carly took it out of the envelope and handed it to him to read. "I don't think she'll sell, but I don't blame her. She'd like me to ask her about some of her other work."

"What do you plan to do?" Brand pushed his empty plate aside and reached over and took an olive from hers.

She slapped the back of his hand lightly and twisted to reach for the jar on the counter. "Take your own, bub," she rebuked him with a teasing grin.

Brand emptied several more onto his plate and replaced the one he'd taken of hers. "Well?" He raised questioning eyes to hers.

"I think I'll write her again. Even if she won't sell the portrait, I'd like to get to know her. Whoever Jutta Hoverson is or whatever she's done doesn't bother me. It's obvious the two of us have a lot in common."

Brand didn't respond directly; instead, his gaze slid to the bouquet she'd tossed on the countertop. His expression was gentle, almost tender. "You'd better put those in water."

Carly's gaze rested on the pink and white carnations and she released her breath slowly. She reached for her cigarettes, suddenly needing one. Her hand was steady as she flicked the lighter and the flame curled around the tip of a cigarette. She exhaled, and a steady stream of smoke penetrated the air. "Take the flowers home with you."

"Why?" He regarded her closely, his expression grim.

"I thought you were paying off Sandra's medical bills."

"What's that got to do with anything?"

"We're friends, remember?" Her voice was low. "Flowers are something you'd bring to impress a date. You don't need to impress me, St. Clair. I'm a friend. I don't ever plan to be anything more."

Brand sat still and quiet, and although he didn't speak, Carly could feel his anger. "I wasn't trying to impress you." His voice was so deep it vibrated. "My intention was more to cheer you, but I can see that I failed." Moving in the oppressive silence that had filled the room, Brand stood, carried his empty plate to the sink and, with suppressed violence, threw the flowers into the garbage can. Carly heard his sigh of disgust. His expression was weary as he regarded her.

"Brand," Carly tried. She hadn't expected him to react so violently.

He ignored her as he moved into the living room. "Thanks for the sandwich," he said before the front door slammed behind him. The explosive sound vibrated off the walls and wrapped its way around Carly's throat, choking off her oxygen supply.

She ground out her half-smoked cigarette and exhaled. "Damn," she emitted harshly and stared at the blank wall.

An hour later, Carly had written a reply to Jutta Hoverson. The second letter was easier to pen than the first had been. Again she mentioned how much she'd enjoyed Jutta's work, and recounted the time she'd visited the Seattle Art Museum in Volunteer Park. She told Jutta that she didn't appreciate the abstract creations, but a friend told her that they were supposedly a lot better than they looked. Rereading that part of the letter caused Carly to smile. Of course, the friend had been Diana, and the comment was typical of Diana's sense of humor.

Carly closed the letter by asking Jutta to send more information about her other paintings. As she took a stamp from the kitchen drawer, she caught sight of the carnations, tossed face down in the garbage can. She paused with the stamp raised to her tongue. The carnations looked forlorn and dejected. Carly pulled them from the can and gently brushed the coffee grounds from their pink and white petals. Having no vase, Carly placed them in the center of the table in the empty olive jar, which served admirably as a holder.

Now Carly regretted her hastily spoken words to Brand. There were better ways of expressing her feelings. But hindsight was twenty-twenty. That was another of Diana's favorite witticisms. Dear God, she missed Diana.

After a restless evening in which her mind refused to concentrate on any project, Carly realized that she wouldn't feel right about anything until she'd apologized to Brand. Humble pie had never been her specialty, but as she recalled, though the initial bite was bitter, the aftertaste was generally sweet. At least she'd be able to go on with her day. And the sooner the apology was made, the better. To take the easy way out and phone him tempted her, but Carly resisted. Instead, she donned a thick cable-knit sweater and drove the distance to Brand's apartment.

Her knock on his door was determined and she waited long enough to wonder if he was home. His truck was outside, but that didn't mean much. She finally heard movement inside the apartment and placed a pink carnation between her teeth before the door was opened. "Peace?" she offered.

"Carly." An unreadable expression clouded Brand's face. "Come in."

Carly removed the flower and attempted to spit out the unpalatable taste of the stem and leaves as she moved inside. "Well?" she questioned, slightly defensive.

Brand moved a hand over his face, as if he thought she might be an apparition. "Well, what?"

"Am I forgiven my cavalier attitude?"

He looked at her blankly, as if he still didn't understand what she was asking. "You mean about the flowers?"

Carly tipped her head to one side. Brand had obviously been asleep and she'd woken him. Things were going from bad to worse. "I'm sorry, I... I didn't know you were in bed."

"Care to join me?" Brand teased softly and brought her into his arms. He inhaled, as if to take in the fresh scent of her. "It's been a long time since I had someone warm to cuddle."

"No." Carly held herself stiff, but she melted against him when his finger traced the smooth line of her jaw. His mere touch had the power to weaken her.

Brand's soft chuckle tingled against the side of her neck as he paused to nuzzle her. "Why don't you put on some coffee while I grab a shirt and shoes?'' He pulled away reluctantly.

Carly's back was to him when Brand entered the kitchen a few moments later. ''My coming today was a gesture of friendship,'' she began, and smiled tightly as she turned. ''I felt bad about what happened at my place. My attitude was wrong. You were being kind and I...''

''Friendship.'' Brand repeated the word as if he found it distasteful. ''I think it's time you woke up to the fact that what I feel for you goes far beyond being pals.''

''But you agreed...'' Carly was having difficulty finding her tongue. ''We aren't even dating.''

The coffee was perking furiously behind her and Brand moved to her side and poured two mugs, carrying them to the table. ''We aren't going to argue about it. If you want to ignore the plain and simple truth, that's up to you.''

The arrogance of the man was too much. ''You think I'm going to fall in love with you,'' she said incredulously.

Brand blew into the side of the ceramic mug before taking a tentative sip. ''If you're honest with yourself, you'll admit you're halfway there as it is.''

Carly slapped one thigh and snickered softly. ''I don't think you're fully awake. You're living in a dream world, fellow.''

Brand shrugged. ''If you say so.''

''I know so.'' Carly sat across from him and cupped her mug with both hands, letting the warmth chase the chill from her blood. "In fact, if that's your attitude, maybe it'd be better if we didn't see one another again. Not at all."

Brand shrugged, giving the impression that either way was fine with him. "Maybe."

Carly laid the palms of both hands on top of the table and half raised herself out of her chair. "Would you please stop it?"

Brand tossed her a look of pure innocence. "I told you I wasn't going to argue with you, Carly. That's exactly what you want, and I refuse to play your games."

"I don't want to fight," she shouted.

"'And if I don't stop, you'll slug me,'" he finished for her with a sarcastic smile.

Closing her eyes, Carly clenched her teeth and groaned. "You know, I'm beginning to think that the rocks in my head would fill the holes in yours."

Brand laughed and reached across the table to take her hand with the intention of bringing it to his lips, but Carly jerked it free.

Undeterred by her rejection, Brand continued, "Why don't you come over here and put your arms around my neck and kiss me the way you've wanted to from the moment you walked in the door?"

Stunned, Carly nearly dropped her mug. It thumped against the table, and hot coffee sloshed over the side. She jumped up to get a rag to catch the liquid before it flowed onto the floor. The color drained from her face as she sopped up the mess. She *had* wanted to kiss him. In the back of her mind, she had formed a picture of her apology being followed by Brand kissing her senseless and carrying her into his bedroom. Dear God. Carly closed her eyes and exhaled sharply.

The sound of Brand pushing back his chair filled her with panic. She had to escape.

"Oh, no, you don't." He spoke softly as his hand caught her shoulder and turned her into his arms.

Struggling was useless. "Brand, no," she pleaded, and then swallowed to control the husky tremor in her voice. "I have to go . . . there's something . . ."

She wasn't allowed to finish as his mouth plundered hers. Her lips parted to protest the invasion, and the instant they did, all gentleness left Brand. His hold tightened as he hungrily devoured her mouth. His hand at the back of her neck increased its pressure, lifting Carly onto the tips of her toes.

If she'd been confused before, it was nothing compared to the deluge of sensations that rocked her now. Her knees were weak, but she felt heady with the strength of her response. She was both assaulted and cradled. Victor and vanquished. Nothing made sense as she surrendered to her swirling desire. Her tongue outlined Brand's mouth and he groaned. He broke off the kiss long enough to move with her to the chair and pull her into a sitting position on his lap.

Their eyes locked, and words became unnecessary. Brand wrapped his hands in her dark hair, directing her mouth to his. She felt his hunger as his mouth and tongue reclaimed hers. Together they strained to satisfy each other. Brand's hands slid beneath her sweater to stroke her bare flesh. The feel of his hand against her back was pleasant and soothing, but when it circled around her midriff and cupped her breast she felt a stirring of something wild and primitive. She broke away and buried her face in the curve of his shoulder.

Apparently sensing her reluctance, Brand moved his hand, but continued to explore her back beneath the sweater. "Don't fight me so hard," he murmured.

Carly sighed thoughtfully. "The way I see it, I'm not fighting near hard enough." She could feel his smile against her temple. "I'm frightened," she whispered after a long moment.

"I know."

"I don't want to fall in love with you," she said painfully.

"I know that too."

Carly's eyes rested on the clean top of the television. "What did you do with Sandra's picture?" He'd put it away, she knew, but she needed to know where.

"It's in a drawer."

Somehow she'd expected him to wince when she mentioned his dead wife, but he didn't. "Top or bottom?"

A hand on each shoulder turned her so that she could look him in the eye. "Bottom."

She lowered her gaze, embarrassed at revealing the depth of her insecurity. "Now," he said, and a hint of firmness stole into his voice. "When are you going to stop running from me?"

"I don't—"

Narrowed, disbelieving eyes forbade her from completing her words. "Carly, look at me. I'm through with this 'we're-not-dating' business. We are *seriously* dating and I won't take no for an answer. Understand?"

She nodded numbly. All the old insecurities bobbed to the surface of her mind, but when Brand put his arms around her they seemed inconsequential. Only when she was alone did they grow ominous and forbidding.

Brand patted the lump of discarded glass in her jeans pocket. "Either you've got a serious problem with your bones or you're sprouting something in your pocket."

Carly smiled and arched her back so she could withdraw the glass. "Here." She gave it to Brand. "I found a treasure."

"Treasure?" He eyed her warily.

"It's as green as an emerald."

"Yes," Brand agreed.

She took it back, rubbed it between the palms of her hands and held it to his face. "And warm as fire."

"Not quite that hot."

"We're imagining here," she chastised playfully. "Now hold it up to the light."

Brand did as she requested. "Yes?"

"See the cracks and lines?"

"So?"

"It's as intriguing as a map. A treasure map," she added. "And I bet you thought this was just a plain old piece of broken glass that time had smoothed."

Brand closed his fingers over the green glass and a sadness suddenly stole over him. "That's the kind of wonder Shawn would discover in this."

"Shawn?" A coldness settled over her even before Brand could answer.

"My son."

"You have children?" The question came out breathlessly, her voice low and wobbly.

"Yes. Shawn and Sara."

Suddenly Carly knew what it must feel like to die.

Chapter Five

Several hours later the knot in her stomach still hadn't relaxed. Even now her breath came in short, painful wisps. Brand had children. Beautiful children. He'd taken their photo from his wallet and Carly had been forced to stare at two blond youngsters. Both Shawn and Sara had been gifted with Sandra's beautiful eyes and Sandra's hair color.

For every second that Carly had studied the picture she'd died a little more. Brand had explained that his children were living with his mother in Oregon, but they'd be joining him in a couple of months once school was out for the summer.

"How old?" Somehow Carly managed to ask the question.

Brand's eyes were proud. That he loved and missed his family was obvious. "Shawn's seven and Sara's five."

Carly nodded and returned the photo.

"You'll like them, Carly."

Brand had sounded so confident, unaware of the turmoil that viciously attacked her.

A few minutes after that, Brand walked her to his front door. "I'll see you tomorrow," he said and gently kissed her brow. "We can talk more about us."

Carly wanted to scream at him that there wasn't anything to discuss, but she held her tongue, realizing an argument would solve nothing.

On the way out the door, Carly's shoe caught on the rug and she stumbled forward. She would have fallen if Brand hadn't caught her.

"Are you okay?"

"Fine," she mumbled, "I'm fine."

Brand knelt at her side and retrieved her shoe. "The heel's broken. I can probably fix it, if you like."

"No, no, it's fine. Don't worry."

The minute Carly was in her apartment, she took off the shoes and threw them both in the garbage. For the first time in recent memory Carly was pleased that Diana wasn't around to witness this latest attack of wastefulness. Yes, the shoes could be repaired. But not for her. Too many times in her life she'd been forced to wear repaired shoes. But not any more. Diana saw her attitude as ridiculous, but Carly considered the cost of new shoes a small price to pay.

* * *

Moon shadows danced across the walls as Carly lay in bed, unable to sleep. It was hours later. Already she was dreading Brand's coming. She had to tell him she wouldn't see him again. Every condition she'd set for their relationship had been broken. He had come right out and told her he wanted more from her than friendship.

The most disturbing thing had been that Brand had known how badly she'd wanted to kiss him. He had been able to see it when she hadn't even admitted it to herself. If she was that easy to decipher, Carly doubted that she could disguise any of her feelings. And she was dangerously close to falling in love with Brandon St. Clair. Placing Sandra, Shawn and Sara out of the picture, Brand could make her feel more of a woman than she had at any other time in her life. The attraction between them was so strong she didn't know if she could fight against the swift current of their mutual awareness.

In the morning, Carly dressed for work. Standing in the kitchen, she was buttering a piece of toast when the discarded loafers caught her eye. Throwing them out was a wasteful, childish action. Having them repaired would be such a little thing. This quirk, this penchant for perfection, was ruining her life. Carly turned her back and ignored the shoes. They were old, worn, and she'd have thrown them out in a few weeks anyway. *But they were comfortable,* her mind returned quickly.

At the front door on her way out, Carly suddenly turned around and went back into the kitchen. She lifted the shoes out of the garbage and set them on the floor. Time. All she needed was time to think things over.

"Morning, George." Carly set her purse on top of her desk and walked across the room to pour herself a cup of coffee.

George had a clipboard in his hand. A deep scowl darkened his face. "Do you remember the Longmeir shipment to Palmer?"

Leaning her hip against her desk, Carly cupped the coffee mug with both hands. "Sure, we trucked that out last week."

George set the clipboard aside. "It didn't arrive."

"What?" Carly straightened. Two days after arriving at Alaska Freight Forwarding, she'd learned that Longmeir was their best and most demanding customer. The mining company had bases throughout the state and depended on Alaska Freight to ship the needed supplies to each site in the most expeditious, most dependable and most economic way. Carly had been the one to decide to truck this latest shipment rather than use rail cars. George had concurred with her suggestion, but the decision had been hers.

"Needless to say, that freight's got to be found. And fast."

Brushing the hair from her forehead, Carly pulled out a desk chair. "I'll get on it right away."

"Do that," George ordered crisply.

By late afternoon Carly had gone through a pack and a half of cigarettes and fifteen cups of coffee. Near closing time she tracked down the lost shipment. The truck driver had delivered it to the wrong camp, but that site had no record of accepting the shipment. There had been foul-ups at both ends—and Charles Longmeir wasn't a man to accept excuses. Carly stayed until everyone else had left for home. She had an idea that once the handler at the other camp inventoried his supplies, they'd be able to verify the location and make the necessary adjustments. However, that couldn't be done until morning. Rotating her neck to ease the tense muscles, Carly couldn't recall a worse Monday.

Letting herself into her apartment, she felt mentally and physically exhausted. George had voiced his displeasure all day. If they lost the Longmeir account, she might as well kiss her job goodbye. George hadn't actually said as much, but the implication was there. To complicate matters, she was due to investigate a large claim on another order that had arrived damaged. Her stomach felt acidy and she could feel the beginnings of a headache prickling at her temple. Little wonder. She hadn't eaten anything since her toast that morning.

The phone rang at seven-thirty, and Carly didn't answer it, certain Brand was at the other end of the line. She didn't feel up to seeing him that night. All she wanted was a tall glass of milk, a hot bath and bed. In that order.

She hadn't finished the milk when someone knocked on her door. Carly didn't need to be told it was Brand.

"Hi." He greeted her with a light brush of his mouth against hers.

Carly was astonished that such a little thing as this brief kiss could affect her, but it did. "Brand, I've had a rotten day. I'm not in the mood for company."

"I know. George told me about the Longmeir shipment." He disregarded her lack of welcome and walked past her into the kitchen, carrying a grocery bag. "I'll only stay a few minutes," he promised. "Now, sit down, put your feet up and relax."

"Brand," Carly moaned, half pleading, half amused. She was still holding the front door open, but he was in her kitchen humming merrily. "Just what do you think you're doing?" she challenged.

"Taking care of you."

Carly closed the door and marched into the kitchen. "I don't need anyone."

Brand was at her stove, a dish towel wrapped around his waist as he cracked fresh eggs against the side of a bowl. "I know that." He didn't look at her as he spoke, and ignored the irritation that coated her voice. "You've been on your own for a long time. But I'm here now."

"Brand, please . . ."

He turned and took her by both shoulders, his eyes holding hers with such warmth that she couldn't resist when he lowered his mouth to hers. His kiss brought her into quick submission. "Now, go relax. I'll call you when dinner is ready."

Carly complied, wondering why she allowed him so much control over her. Leaning her head against the back of the love seat, her eyes drooped closed. The sound of Brand's humming as he worked lulled her into a light, pleasant sleep. Eyes shut, Carly's mind followed Brand's movements in the kitchen. She heard him whipping the eggs and chopping something on the cutting board; she heard the sizzle of the butter when he added it to the hot skillet. That sound was followed by another she couldn't identify, then finally she heard the eggs being stirred in the pan and bread being lowered in the toaster. Delicious smells drifted toward her, and Carly realized how hungry she was.

"Dinner's ready," Brand called and he stood behind her chair, waiting to pull it out as she approached.

Her eyes widened at the sight of the appealing omelet. Melted cheese and pieces of onion and green pepper oozed from the sides of his tantalizing masterpiece. "Wow," she said as she sat down. "You never told me you could cook, like this."

"There wasn't any reason to mention it before now. I've been on my own long enough to learn the fundamentals."

Carly took the first bite and shook her head in wonder. "This is fantastic."

"I didn't think you'd want dinner out."

"After a day like today, all I want is a hot bath and bed."

A mischievous grin curved the edges of Brand's mouth. "If that's an invitation, I accept."

The sexual banter between them seemed to grow more pointed with every meeting. Carly shook her head forcefully. "No, it wasn't," she announced primly.

She finished her meal and carried the plate to the sink. "How did you know I hadn't eaten?" Carly asked, not turning around. Most people would have had their dinner before now. A glance at her slim wristwatch confirmed that it was nearly nine.

His eyes grew warm. "Because I'm beginning to know you, Carly Grieves. You don't eat when you're upset."

"But I smoke like a chimney."

"Yes, and drink a ton of coffee. It's a wonder you haven't gotten an ulcer."

Making busywork at the sink, Carly hoped that Brand would take the silent message and leave. The feelings she'd battled during the weekend returned. She wanted him to go, and at the same time, inexplicably, she needed him to stay.

"Aren't you going to thank me for dinner?" he asked softly, coming to her side. He slipped his arms around her waist from behind and kissed the gentle slope of her neck.

Carly went still as she breathed in the clean male scent of him. "Thank you, Brand." Her voice was barely above a whisper.

"I was hoping you'd have other ways of expressing your appreciation," he whispered and gently nibbled on the lobe of her ear.

"No, I don't." She prayed he couldn't detect the thread of breathlessness in her voice.

His hand stole beneath her sweater and slid across her ribs as his mouth sought and found the sensitive areas on her neck. Carly tilted her head to one side, loving the delicious sensations he brought to life within her. When his hand cupped her breast, she all but cried out at the unexpected pleasure. A trembling weakness shook her and she melted against him, her softness reveling in the touch of his hard length. Brand turned her into his arms and she linked her hands at the base of his neck.

"Kiss me, Carly," he ordered huskily.

She defied him with her eyes, not wanting to give in to him. Not so easily. Her pride—and so much more— was at stake. She couldn't allow herself to become involved with this man.

Their gazes locked in a silent battle of wills. His dark eyes were narrowed with demand. Unable to meet the command in his look, Carly's gaze slid to his mouth. His lips were slightly parted, eager. And Carly couldn't deny him . . . couldn't deny herself.

Finally she obliged, her mouth slanting over his, kissing him with a thoroughness that left them both weak and breathless. He clung to her as if he was afraid to let her go.

"Are you happy now?" she asked, rubbing her cheek along the side of his jaw in a feline caress. The abrasive feel of his unshaven beard against her skin's smoothness was strangely welcome.

"No." He kissed the corner of her mouth, seeking more, but Carly successfully forestalled him. "Brand, I want you to teach me to fly."

"What?" He stiffened and pulled his head back to study her.

"You heard me."

"But why?"

"Why not?" she quizzed.

"I can think of a hundred reasons."

"I thought you said you wanted me to look at your accounting books."

"You know I do." He broke away from her and strode to the other side of the kitchen, his face tight and troubled. The mute suggestion that he couldn't think with her in his arms pleased her. He paused and folded his arms over his chest.

"I suggest we trade labor," Carly continued.

Brand didn't look pleased, although he appeared to be mulling the suggestion over. "You'll have to read several books."

"I'm not illiterate," Carly challenged with a light laugh. "I'll have you know I read books all the time."

Brand's glance was wry and he returned evenly, "Yes, I imagine you do."

"Well?" The idea made perfect sense to her.

Brand shrugged and walked into the living room to pick up the *TV Guide*. "I suppose," he said and turned on the television.

Carly wasn't fooled. Brand didn't like her idea, but she'd show him how much sense it made. The afternoon they'd spent in the air had only whetted her appetite for more. Soaring through the air, viewing the world from the clouds would be a magical experience. And having Brand teach her would be the most feasible way.

"Come and watch this movie with me," Brand said. A trace of amusement sparkled from his eyes, and the corners of his mouth turned up.

"What's so funny?"

"Nothing." He returned his attention to the television. His hand moved to cup her shoulder when she sat down beside him.

The movie was one Carly had seen, but she didn't say anything. It felt warm and pleasant to be held by Brand. His touch was gentle, yet almost impersonal.

He didn't leave until after the eleven o'clock news, kissing her lightly at the front door. "Are you sure you don't want to thank me for dinner again?" he whispered against the soft wisps of hair that grew at her temple. "I could easily be persuaded to accept your gratitude."

His voice was only half teasing, and Carly knew it. "Next time I'll throw you out the door," she declared with mock severity.

"I'll see you tomorrow night—it's your turn to cook," he said with a self-assured chuckle.

"My turn..." She had no intention of seeing him tomorrow.

"Yes. I'll bring the ledgers over after work."

"Brand, I told you before I'm not much of a cook. I eat a lot of green olives and chocolate." Carly crossed her arms over her breast to chase away a sudden chill.

"Don't worry about it. Until tomorrow," he said, and gave her a lingering kiss to seal the promise.

Carly's spirits lifted the next morning when she got a call confirming that the lost shipment was indeed at the wrong warehouse, as she'd pinpointed. The handler promised to have the equipment en route to the proper camp that afternoon, by company truck.

George looked as relieved as Carly felt. "None of this trouble was your doing," he said by way of apologizing. "And, listen, I've been thinking about that wedding you said you wanted to attend."

Carly's hand tightened around her pencil. When she'd approached George about Diana's wedding, he'd been less than enthusiastic about giving her the three days off. He hadn't answered her, but had mumbled something under his breath about no vacation time being due her until next summer. His expression had been so forbidding that she'd let the matter drop.

"Yes," she said, holding her breath.

"Go ahead. Just be sure your assignments are complete and all the claims have been taken care of."

"I will," Carly responded evenly, then grinned up at the white-haired man. Over the weeks she'd come to overlook his gruff exterior. "Thanks, George."

"Just make sure your friends understand that I won't have you gallivanting to Seattle every time one of them decides to get married."

"I wouldn't dream of asking." Lowering her head, Carly tried unsuccessfully to disguise a smile.

"When will you be leaving?" George flipped open the appointment book on the top of his desk.

"I'd like to leave a week from Thursday." She waited for a flurry of complaints, but none came.

"Fine. When can I expect you back?"

"The following Tuesday—Wednesday at the latest."

George didn't blink. Carly could hardly believe it. She would phone Diana the minute she got home... oh, darn, Brand was coming over for dinner. And she couldn't cook. He *knew* that. Well, a couple of TV dinners would discourage him. Brand seemed to be under the impression that just because they were trading skills, they would be seeing one another every night. She hadn't made this proposition as an excuse to see more of him—but he'd learn that soon enough.

During the drive from work to her apartment, Carly felt the faint stirrings of guilt. After a hard day, Brand would need something more than a frozen dinner, and she wasn't capable of putting together anything more than soup and a sandwich. Frustrated with herself because she cared about what he ate, she took a short side trip to the local fried chicken place.

Brand was at the door only minutes after she arrived home. His arms were loaded with books. "Whatever you're cooking smells good."

"I didn't cook anything," she announced coolly as she set two plates out on the table.

"You don't sound very relaxed. Did you find the freight?"

"I located it. And it was exactly where I'd assumed it had to be," she answered absently, neatly folding two paper napkins and placing them beside the plastic forks.

"Are you going to kiss me hello or will I be forced to take you in my arms and—"

Carly leaned over and brushed her lips against his cheek in a sisterly manner. "Go ahead and put that stuff on the coffee table."

For a second it looked as if Brand was going to argue with her. He hadn't appreciated her miserly kiss and his look said as much.

"Go on," she urged, struggling to hide her satisfied smile. "Everything here's ready." She surveyed the table. Fried chicken, mashed potatoes, giblet gravy, coleslaw and fresh biscuits. She hadn't eaten a meal like this since Diana and Barney had taken her out for a going-away celebration.

"I'll be back in a minute." Brand set the books aside and returned a moment later with a large box.

"Good grief, what's that?"

He glanced sheepishly at the department-store box under his arm. "Receipts, canceled checks and the like."

"A whole box?"

Brand nodded, slightly abashed. "I'll help if you want."

She'd been party to his kind of assistance in the past. "No, thanks." She raised one hand in defense. "You'd only mess up my system." *And my mind,* she added silently.

They talked as they ate. Brand explained that he would be around town most of that week, but he had some distance flying coming up in the early part of the next. Carly listened politely, thinking that he was talking to her as he would a wife. The idea terrorized her. She had hoped to pull away from Brand, but her life became more entwined with his every day. The crazy thing was that it was her own doing. She was the one who'd suggested they trade skills.

"Speaking of traveling," she said, wiping her fingers clean on a yellow napkin. "I'm going to be doing some of my own. I'll be leaving next week for Seattle."

"Any special reason?" His smile seemed an effort.

"Diana's getting married." Her eyes brightened with an inner glow of happiness for her friend. "I'm booking my flight for a week from Thursday morning." The wedding was scheduled for Friday night, but Carly wanted to be there early enough to soothe any attacks of nerves.

"And you'll be back..."

"The following Tuesday. Brand..." She took a deep breath. "What do you think of the idea of me stopping in Purdy and meeting Jutta Hoverson? It wouldn't be out of my way. Diana would let me use her car. I'd really like to meet her."

"Why?"

She glanced away, not wanting him to see how much the idea excited her. "Several reasons."

"Are you hoping that she'll sell you the painting?"

The question unaccountably provoked her. "No, course not. That's not it at all. I . . . I just want to see what she looks like, that's all. I'm sorry I asked." Carly twisted her half-smoked cigarette with unnecessary force. "Not everyone has ulterior motives, you know."

Laughter burst from Brand. "Now, don't get all shook up. I was only curious."

Carly removed a piece of lint from her wool skirt. "I think you should remember something, St. Clair." Her words were clipped and impatient. "I have more in common with Jutta Hoverson than I'll ever have with you."

Brand's mouth slanted with his apparent effort to suppress an angry retort. "I won't fight with you."

"Is this what you did every time Sandra had a complaint? Did you refuse to fight with her, too?"

"Leave Sandra out of this."

"No," she snapped.

Silence hung between them like a dark, gray thundercloud. Electricity filled the room, ready to arc at the slightest provocation.

Rising, Brand rammed his hands deep within his jeans pockets. "Sandra and I fought just like every couple does, but I won't fight with you, Carly."

"Why?" She felt like shouting at him, but when she spoke her voice was low and filled with frustration.

"Because it's the excuse you're looking for to shove me out of your life. I've been chipping away for too long at the wall you've built around yourself to blow it over a stupid argument." He paused and rubbed his eyes. "I was in Oregon last week."

Brand had been gone almost the entire week and she'd assumed it was on business. He didn't need to tell her what had drawn him to his home. His children were there.

"For the first time since Sandra died, I found I could look at my son and daughter and not feel the gut-wrenching pain of having lost their mother. You've done that for me, Carly."

"No," she mumbled and shook her head from side to side.

"Yes, damn it. Now, listen to me. If you weren't running so hard from me you'd see what's right in front of your nose."

Jumping up, Carly took Brand's plate from the table and carried it to the sink. She didn't want to look at him, she didn't want to hear him. Filling the sink with water, she hoped to drown out his words.

"I took Shawn and Sara to Cannon Beach with me. Sandra loved the beach," he continued, ignoring Carly's frenzied movements. "I hadn't been there since she died."

Carly's fingers gripped the edge of the sink as she closed her eyes, silently screaming for him to stop. She wasn't a part of his life. He had no reason to tell her these things. She shouldn't be that important to him.

"I'd always thought, whenever I went back, that I wouldn't be able to stand looking at the ocean again. Sandra had loved it so much. But nothing had changed . . . even though I guess maybe I thought it would. But the wind blew and the sea rumbled and the shorebirds soared as they always have."

"Please," Carly pleaded. "I don't want to hear this."

"But you're going to, even if it means I have to force you to listen."

Without turning around, Carly knew that Brand's mouth had tightened into a grim line. Arguing would be useless.

Brand began again. "One afternoon, while Shawn and Sara were playing in the sand, I stood with the wind blowing against me and closed my eyes. A picture of Sandra filled my mind. But not in the ordinary sense of remembering. She was there smiling, happy as she'd always been at the beach, smelling of wildflowers and sunshine. As long as I kept my eyes closed she was there with me and the children. The only sounds were those of the children, and the gentle whisper of the wind. But when I strained I thought for an instant I could hear the faint call of Sandra's laughter."

Tears filled Carly's eyes and she blinked in a desperate effort to forestall their flow. "Don't," she murmured entreatingly, "please don't do this to me." Her mind was filled with the image of this proud man standing on the beach with the wind buffeting against him, communicating with his dead wife.

"You don't understand," Brand said softly. "For the first time since she died, I felt her presence instead of her absence. For two years my memories of her have been tied up with the agony of her death. I looked out at the ocean and felt a sense of life again. That desolate darkness I'd wrapped myself in was gone. The time had come to go back. Back to the world. Back to people. Back to my children. But mostly back to you."

Carly wiped the moisture from her face with both hands.

"It was you who brought back to life feelings I had assumed were long dead. You, Carly." He moved so that he was standing directly behind her. "I'm falling in love with you. From the moment I walked into your office I knew there was something special about you. You've hidden from me, dodged me, fought me. But the time's come, my sweet Carly, for you to look out over the ocean and choose life."

Her lips went dry and she moistened them. Fresh tears burned for release, but she held them back as she'd always done, her throat aching with the effort. Turning, she slipped her arms around his waist and buried her face against his broad chest. Brand wrapped his arms around her so tightly that for a moment she couldn't breathe. He needed her; Carly could feel it. His breathing was slow and ragged, as though it was an effort for him to hold back the emotion.

"I guess this means we're dating," she said after a long moment.

Her words were followed by the low rumble of Brand's laughter. "Yes, I guess you could say that."

"Brand..." She hesitated. "All this frightens me."

"I know. I was afraid too."

"But you're not anymore?"

"No." His hand traced the outline of her face, tilting her chin so that he could meet her troubled gaze. "Not anymore."

"Why..." She swallowed at the painful knot blocking her larynx. "Why didn't you tell me about your children?"

"I had trouble even talking about them. They were part of the life I'd left behind."

"But you said they're coming to Alaska soon."

"As soon as school's out. I told them about you."

Carly stiffened. "What did you say?"

He kissed the tip of her nose. "I told them I had a special friend that I was beginning to love just as I loved their mother."

"Oh, Brand, I wish you hadn't," she whispered, her voice trembling.

He ignored her, but his grip tightened, as if he was afraid she'd bolt and run as she'd done so many times in the past. "A funny little friend who climbed mountains and jumped out of airplanes and liked to eat green olives and chocolate."

"And... and what did they say?"

Brand laughed and mussed the top of her head with his chin. "Shawn wanted to know if you'd take him with you the next time you decide to climb Mount Rainier. And Sara was more concerned about whether or not you liked Smurfs.''

"What?''

"Little blue cartoon people. Apparently, anyone who likes Smurfs is a defender of truth and justice and worthy of my attention.''

"Whatever happened to Superman?''

"I don't think Sara would trust any man who'd wear blue tights.''

Carly's smile was shaky and the effort it cost her to make it drained her.

Sandra's children would be joining him soon. A sense of unrest attacked her. True, she could climb mountains and jump out of airplanes, but the thought of meeting these two children filled her with undescribable terror.

Chapter Six

Brand came into Carly's office yawning on Thursday afternoon. "Lord, I'm bushed," he declared as he sat down on George's desk chair. "I don't know, Carly. Someone's changed the rules in the last ten years."

Rising, she poured him a cup of steaming coffee. "What do you mean?"

"I'm too old for these late nights. I used to be able to get by on four or five hours sleep. But I'm too old for this."

They'd been together every night. They talked, watched television, went for long walks and discussed flying. Not once had Brand left Carly's before midnight.

Responding to his tiredness, she put her hand over her own mouth and yawned loudly.

"I'll be late tonight," Brand said after taking the first sip from the coffee cup.

"Good," Carly returned with a lazy smile. "That'll give me a chance to go over those flying theory books you brought me."

Brand lowered his gaze, but not before Carly saw his frown. Although he hadn't said anything to discourage her, it was obvious he didn't want her to learn to fly. He'd know soon enough, Carly mused now, that she was her own woman. Diana had often reacted with the same show of reluctance at Carly's adventurous inclinations. Carly could almost hear her friend's protestations about her latest interest.

"Do you want me to have something ready for you to eat?" The offer was more selfish than generous; Carly realized how much she looked forward to their time together in the evenings. Not that they did a lot of social things. Brand's finances wouldn't allow for much of that. Maybe once a week, but certainly not every night. Brand was taking her to dinner Friday night and Carly had felt less nervous when the captain of the football team had asked her for a date in high school!

"I may not be there until after ten," Brand warned.

"No problem. And you know better than to expect a three-course meal."

Setting his empty mug aside, Brand stood and kissed her on the cheek. "I'll see you later," he promised, his voice low and husky.

George returned to the office just as Brand left. Carly stood at the window until Brand had climbed into his car and was gone.

"You two have been seeing a lot of one another, haven't you?"

Carly's answer was a nod. Her private life had nothing to do with the office and she wasn't going to elaborate on her relationship with Brand to satisfy George's curiosity.

"He's a rare man, Brand St. Clair."

She could feel George's contemplative gaze. Her boss had seen the look on her face—and knew the cause. "Yes, he is," Carly agreed, and turned back to her desk.

"He's driven himself hard. But he looks more relaxed now then I can ever remember," George continued.

Carly said nothing, not wanting to encourage him.

"I don't suppose you could say anything to him about becoming a full-time pilot for Alaska Freight Forwarding, could you?"

Mercifully, the phone rang, so Carly didn't have to answer George. By the time she'd replaced the receiver, her employer had left the office.

When Carly returned to the empty apartment that evening, she felt restless. Usually Brand arrived shortly after she did. Now, for the first time in days, the evening stretched out ahead of her. The thought shocked Carly. A couple of times she found herself glancing at her watch and mentally calculating how long it would be until Brand arrived. This was exactly what she hadn't wanted.

Bit by bit, Brand had wiggled his way into her life. She did his bookkeeping, he was teaching her how to fly an airplane. Their evenings were spent in each other's company. Sometimes he dropped by the office unexpectedly, for no more reason than to have a cup of coffee and chat for a few minutes. Now, a day without spending some time with Brand would seem unnatural. She had tried to write to Diana about these fears concerning her relationship with Brand, but ended up throwing all of her attempts away. What she was experiencing came from the heart, not from the mind. And although she loved her friend, there were certain things even Diana couldn't be expected to understand.

There was so much she didn't know about Brand, and yet she knew everything she would ever need to. Nothing in his life had ever been done halfheartedly. Only a man who loved with such intensity could grieve the way he had for Sandra. Only a man with as much insight and understanding of her personality could be as patient as Brand. For all that he was, she loved him. The realization came to her gently, warm and secure, kindling a fire that glowed. She did love Brand. What she didn't know was whether or not her love for him was strong enough to overcome the fears and anxieties ingrained on her conscience since childhood.

The FCC flight manual was balanced on her bent knee and the television was on with the volume turned down when Brand knocked lightly against her door.

"Hi." She greeted him with a hug. "Are you hungry?"

"Starved," he groaned, and pulled her into his arms. "But before you go into the kitchen I expect a proper greeting. None of those miserly kisses you seem to be so fond of giving me."

Smiling seductively, Carly slid her hands up his chest and allowed them to rest on the masculine curve of his shoulders. "Remember," she whispered huskily as she fit her body intimately to his, "you asked for this." She kissed one corner of his mouth and then the other. Then, she outlined the contour of his lips with her tongue, darting it in and out of his mouth with a teasing action that affected her as much as it did Brand.

His hands began to caress her back and buttocks in an unhurried exploration as his mouth opened to hers, taking the role of aggressor. His lips parted hers with the probing insistence of his tongue. Carly clung to him, drained of her strength.

They broke apart, each gasping for air.

"A few more of those and I won't be responsible for what happens," he murmured breathlessly.

All the blood flowed from her face. The point in their relationship was fast approaching when kissing would satisfy neither of them. Carly knew that Brand was seriously considering taking her to his bed. But he seemed to be delaying it, apparently as nervous about it as she.

"Let me get your dinner." Hastily, Carly pulled away. She could feel Brand's smile right between her shoulder blades. He was assuming she was running again. He was right.

Happy—perhaps happier than she'd ever been at any time in her life—Carly worked in her small kitchen as Brand leafed through the newspaper. She built him a three-tiered sandwich, piling each piece of bread high with meat from the local deli, adding sliced tomatoes and cut pickles. She topped her creation with a giant green olive that was speared with a toothpick. Then she adorned the plate with potato chips and proudly carried her masterpiece in—only to discover that Brand was asleep on her sofa.

Carly toyed with the idea of waking him, but he looked relaxed and so peaceful that she couldn't.

Returning to the kitchen, Carly bit into a crunchy potato chip and covered the sandwich with plastic wrap. He could eat it tomorrow. Leaning against the counter, Carly yawned.

She tucked an extra pillow under Brand's head and covered him with a spare blanket. The temptation was strong to linger at his side, to make an excuse to touch him. Her fingers flexed with the desire to brush the thick, dark hair from his forehead. But such an action might wake him, and she didn't want to risk that.

An hour later the flight manual could no longer hold her wandering attention. Time and again her gaze slid from the fine print on the page to the sleeping

figure across from her. If Brand hoped to bore her
with dull reading, he was succeeding, but she wouldn't
let him know that. A lot of what she'd gone over tonight might as well have been in a foreign language.
What she needed was a *pre*-preflight instruction manual. But she wouldn't give up. Now she was more determined than ever to get her pilot's license.

She hesitated in the lighted doorway of her room,
watching the moon shadows surround Brand. Realizing that she loved Brand was one thing; what she was
going to do about it was another. So many questions
remained unanswered. Most important were the ones
neither of them had voiced.

When Carly woke the next morning, Brand was
gone. A note was propped on the table apologizing for
his lack of manners. He assured her that his falling
asleep didn't have anything to do with her company,
but only the fact that thirty-three years were taking
their toll. He promised to take her to dinner that evening and asked her to wear her best dress because they
were going to do the town. His hurried postscript
mentioned that the sandwich had been fantastic.

Carly sat with a glass of juice and a plate of toast as
she reread every word of his note twenty times. The
sensation she'd felt upon discovering it was as profound as if Brand had written her a poetic love letter.
Perhaps she was suffering a second adolescence. Lord,
she hoped not. The first one had been difficult
enough.

At the stroke of five, Carly was out the office door. She wanted to luxuriate in a scented bath and be beautiful and alluring when Brand arrived.

The phone was ringing when she walked through the apartment door.

"Hello." Her voice was singsongy with happiness.

"Carly, I'm going to be late."

"Brand, where are you?" The line sounded as if it were long distance.

"Lake Iliamna."

"Where?" He might as well have said Timbuktu.

"The largest lake in Alaska. There's a lodge here."

"Oh." That didn't mean anything to her. "I take it you're using the float plane."

Brand's low chuckle warmed her blood. "The woman's a genius."

"When should I expect you?"

"Honey, I don't know. It could be hours yet."

The endearment rolled off his tongue seemingly without thought, and Carly wondered if that was a name he'd called Sandra. She pushed the thought from her mind forcefully. She couldn't, she *wouldn't* allow Brand's dead wife to haunt their relationship. Not any more than she already did.

"Carly, you're terribly quiet all of a sudden. Are you angry?"

She jerked herself from her musings. "Of course not. Listen, Brand, would you rather cancel the whole thing? I don't mind. We can go out to dinner another time."

"No," he returned. "I want to see you. Hell, I *need* to see you. That is, if you don't mind waiting."

"No," she whispered softly. "I don't mind."

By eleven, Carly was yawning and rubbing her eyes to keep from going to sleep. An old rerun of "Saturday Night Live" was the only thing that kept her from drifting into a welcome slumber.

Brand arrived at midnight. "Carly, I'm sorry," he said the moment she opened the door. "I came right from the airport. Give me another half hour to go home and change. I'll be back as soon as I can."

"We can't go out now." Carly knew what it had taken for him to offer. One look at the fatigue in his eyes was all she needed to see that he was extremely tired. "Nothing's open," she reasoned in a soft voice.

"We'll find something," he assured her, but not too strenuously.

"Nonsense. I'll let you do your magic with eggs and we can eat here. You're exhausted."

His arms brought her into his embrace even with his eyes closed. "I can't argue with you there. It's been a long day."

"What time did you wake up?" He'd spent at least part of the night on her sofa.

"Three. Which was a good thing, since I was due to take off from the airport at four."

"Good heavens, you've been up nearly twenty-four hours."

Brand's responding smile was faltering. "Don't remind me. Tell me about your day."

"There's not much to tell. I got a letter from Jutta Hoverson. She wrote me the day my letter arrived, which makes me feel good."

"What did she have to say?"

"Not much. She's doing some charcoal sketches. The painting of the child was her first oil work. Unbelievable, isn't it?" Not expecting an answer, Carly sat Brand down in the kitchen while she fished leftovers from the refrigerator. "And I phoned Diana to tell her what time my flight would be landing in Seattle. She's too calm about this wedding business. It won't surprise me if she tries to cancel the whole thing at the last minute."

Carly set a tall glass of milk in front of Brand. "Drink," she ordered. "I'll whip up something in a jiffy."

It surprised her that Brand didn't fall asleep in her kitchen chair. After he'd downed some dinner, she led him to the front door. His good-night kiss was as gentle as it was sweet. "I'll phone you tomorrow," he promised. He was making several short flights on Saturday, but couldn't invite her along because he was scheduled to fly crew into camps and there wouldn't be any space in the plane for her.

Carly spent Saturday morning shopping for a dress for Diana's wedding. Although she spent several hours browsing, she couldn't find what she wanted. Problem was, she wasn't sure what she was looking for. But she knew she'd recognize it when she did find it. Shopping had never been her forte and she decided to leave it until she arrived in Seattle. Diana would know exactly where to go.

The rest of the afternoon was spent answering Jutta's short letter. The woman hadn't said much. Few personal details were given in the note. Carly had no idea of her age or background. In her reply, she explained that there was a possibility that she would be able to visit Jutta the following week. She mentioned that she'd like to look at the charcoals then.

With the letter finished, Carly glanced at her watch, surprised to see that it was dinnertime. Not having heard from Brand, Carly assumed that it would be another late night for him.

He showed up around nine, declined her offer of something to eat, and promptly fell asleep on her sofa. This time Carly decided to wake him. Enough was enough. She wouldn't be used like this.

"Brand." Her hand on his shoulder shook him lightly awake.

He bolted upright and blinked. "What happened? Did I fall asleep again?"

Arms crossed, Carly paced the floor in front of the sofa, unsure how to express her frustration.

"What's wrong?" He was awake enough to recognize that she was upset.

"Plenty, and—and don't tell me that you don't want to argue, because this time you're listening to me. Understand?"

Brand wiped a hand across his eyes and nodded. A wary look narrowed his brow as his eyes followed her quick, pacing steps.

Without preamble, Carly began. "I won't be a pit stop in your life, Brand. Maybe some women can live like that, but I'm not one of them. I want to talk to you when you're not so tired that you're rummy. And when I leave the room I want to come back and find you awake."

"A pit stop?" Brand repeated blankly. "Carly, it's not that. Seeing you, being with you is more important to me than anything."

"Then why am I stuck with the leftovers of your life?" The hurt in her eyes was impossible to hide.

He rose with the intention of taking her in his arms, but Carly wasn't in any mood to be kissed into submission as had happened in the past. She sidestepped him easily. "Go home, Brand. Get a decent night's sleep, and maybe we can talk later."

Sitting back down on the couch, Brand rested his elbows on his knees. He folded his hands together with his index fingers forming a small triangle. "I don't want to leave. We need to talk this out." His eyes showed the strain of the past week.

"As far as I can see, there's nothing more to say. I understand why you work the hours you do." She took the chair opposite him. "You can't start a new life with me or anyone else while Sandra's medical expenses are hanging over your head...."

"I paid those off six months ago," he announced in a tight whisper.

"Then why are you pushing yourself like this?"

He didn't answer; instead, he stood and walked to the far side of the room. He paused with his back to her and smoothed the hair along the side of his head. "You're right, Carly. You deserve more than what I've been giving you." His look was sober as he turned, his eyes searching hers. "I love you, Carly. I thought those feelings within me had died with Sandra. But I was wrong." His voice was a hoarse whisper. "I love you, my sweet Carly."

Brand didn't need to tell her that he'd only said those words to one other woman in his life. Carly's fingers were trembling so badly that she clenched them into fists at her sides. The long nails cut deep indentations into her palms. Everything that she wanted and everything that she feared was staring her in the face.

"Well?" Brand was waiting for some kind of reaction.

"Thank you," she whispered, her voice so tight it was hardly recognizable. "I'll always treasure that."

"But you don't know how you feel about me?" Brand returned. His face was rigid.

"I . . . know what I feel." Swallowing was difficult.

"And?"

"You're waiting for me to declare my undying love. That's what you want, isn't it?" She was shouting unreasonably because she was afraid, and striking out was a natural defense.

"Only if that's what you feel." Everything about Brand softened, as if he recognized the turmoil taking place within her heart.

"All right, I love you! Are you happy?" she cried out on a sob. Her whole body was shaking.

"I'm not, if it makes you so miserable."

"It's not that." Lord, she was going to cry. Her throat ached with the effort to suppress the tears.

"Carly, I want to marry you."

"No." The denial was torn from her in shocked dismay. This was the one thing she'd feared the most. Tears slid over the thick dam of her lashes and scalded her cheeks. A hand covered her mouth as she shook her head violently from side to side. "I can't, Brand. I won't marry you."

"Why not?"

There wasn't any explanation that made sense, even to herself. How could she possibly hope to make him understand? "You...you had Sandra. You have children." Her voice wobbled and she tried desperately to control its quivering, but failed.

"What's that got to do with anything?"

Carly moved into the kitchen and picked up the low-heeled loafer from beside the garbage pail. "I'm throwing these away because...because there was never enough money for me as a child and everything had to be fixed and repaired until it was beyond rescuing. I don't want that anymore."

"Carly, you're not making any sense."

"I don't expect you to understand. But I am what I am. You've been married and you've loved." She swallowed down the hurt. "I want to be a man's first love. I want a man to feel for me what you did for Sandra."

"Carly, I do."

"But I want to be your first love," Carly cried. "Don't you understand? All my life I've been forced to take someone else's leftovers. I've always been second and I won't be again, not with a husband. Not with a man.'' Brand looked as if he might come closer to her and she held out a hand to warn him to stay away. ''You have beautiful children, Brand. A boy and a girl. Don't you see? I can't give you anything you don't already have. You've had a wife. You have children.''

The grimness of pain returned to his eyes. ''Then what do you suggest we do?''

''Must we do anything?''

''Yes,'' he shouted, then repeated softly, ''yes. When two people love as strongly as we do, they must.''

Carly lowered her eyes under the intensity of his. ''I don't know what to do, Brand,'' she said, her voice low and throbbing. ''Maybe we could be...'' The word stuck in her throat. ''Lovers.''

A wry smile slanted Brand's mouth as he shook his head. ''Maybe that kind of relationship would satisfy some men. But not me. I've never done anything halfway in my life.'' His pause demanded that she meet his gaze. ''There's so much more that I want from you than a few stolen hours in bed. What I feel goes beyond the physical satisfaction your body will give mine. I want you by my side to build a new life here in Alaska.''

''Please,'' Carly pleaded, ''don't say any more.''

Brand ignored her. ''Together we can give Shawn and Sara the family life they crave. And, God willing, we'll have more children.''

The pain she was inflicting on them both was like a knife blade slicing into her heart. "No. I'm sorry...so sorry. I can't."

He took a step toward her and Carly backed up against the kitchen counter, unable to retreat further.

"You're reacting with your emotions."

She glared at him, wanting him to give her some insight she didn't already have. "None of this makes sense to you. I realize that. I'm not sure I can even fully understand it myself. All I know is what I feel. I won't be a secondhand wife and a secondhand mother."

"Carly..."

"No." She shook her head forcefully. "We've said everything that's important. Rehashing the same arguments won't solve a thing."

He clenched and unclenched his hands with frustration and anger.

"Please," she whispered in soft entreaty. "We're both tired."

Wordlessly, Brand turned, grabbed his jacket from the back of the sofa and left. When the door closed behind him, Carly began to shake with reaction. If it wasn't so tragic, she'd laugh. Brand was so far ahead of her in this relationship. He wanted to marry her—and she had gone only as far as admitting they were dating.

It was nearly two a.m. before Carly went to bed. She knew she wouldn't sleep, and she lay waiting until exhaustion overtook her troubled thoughts. Tomorrow was soon enough. Maybe tomorrow some clear solution would present itself. Tomorrow...

But the morning produced more doubts than reassurances. Loving someone didn't automatically make everything right. And, yes, she loved Brand. But Diana was right, as she almost always was, about Carly. Brand and Carly were two wounded people who had found one another. The immediate attraction that had sparked between them wasn't physical, but spiritual.

When Carly hadn't heard from Brand by Monday afternoon, she realized that he was giving her the room she needed to think things through. His actions proved more than words the depth of his love. Arguing with her would do nothing but frustrate them both.

At any rate, on Thursday morning she would be leaving for Seattle and Diana's wedding. With all the stress Diana was under, Carly couldn't unload her problems on her friend, but at least she would have some time away, close to the only people she had ever considered real family. And Carly needed that.

Tuesday morning, at about ten, Carly heard the familiar sound of Brand's car pulling up outside the office building. Her hand clenched the pencil she was holding tightly, but a smile was frozen on her face when he walked through the door.

"Hello, Carly." He was treating her politely, like a stranger.

"Hi." Her lips felt so stiff she could barely speak.

"You're leaving this week, aren't you?"

He knew exactly when she was going, but Carly played his game. "Thursday morning."

He sauntered over to the coffeepot, and poured himself a cup. Without looking at her, seemingly intent on his task, he spoke. "Will you go out to dinner with me Wednesday night?"

"Yes." There was no question of refusing. The breathing space he'd given her hadn't resolved her dilemma. If anything, she felt more troubled than before. "I'd enjoy that."

He nodded, and for the first time since entering her office, smiled. "I've missed you."

"Me too," she whispered.

Brand took a sip of his coffee. "Where's George?" he asked, suddenly all business.

"In the warehouse." She cocked her head to one side, indicating the area to her right.

"I'll pick you up at seven," he announced, his hand on the doorknob.

"Fine." He was gone and Carly relaxed.

Wednesday evening, with her suitcases packed and ready for the morning flight, Carly dabbed perfume at the pulse points behind her ears and at her wrists. The dress she wore was the most feminine one she owned, a frothy pink thing that wasn't really her. Diana had insisted she buy it, and in a moment of whimsy Carly had done just that. She wasn't sure why she'd chosen to wear it for her dinner date with Brand tonight. But she'd given up analyzing her actions.

Promptly at seven, Brand was at her door. He looked uncomfortable in the dark suit he wore. His hair was cut shorter than she could remember seeing it, and he smelled faintly of musk and spice.

They took one look at each other and broke into wide smiles that hovered on the edge of outright laughter.

"Are we going to act like polite strangers or are we going to be ourselves?" Brand arched one dark brow with his query.

Carly toyed with her answer. If they remained in the roles for which they'd dressed, there was a certain safety. "I don't know," she answered honestly. "If I return to 'Carly, the Confused Woman in Love,' then the evening could be a disaster."

"I, for one, have always courted disaster." He ran his finger down her cheek and cupped the underside of her face before kissing her lightly. "And so have you," he added.

Warm, swirling sensations came at her from all sides and Carly had to restrain herself from wrapping her arms around his neck and kissing Brand the way they both wanted.

He took her to the most expensive restaurant in town and ordered a bottle of vintage Chablis.

"Brand," Carly giggled, leaning across the table. "You can't afford this."

His mouth tightened, but Carly could see that he was amused and hadn't taken offense. What was the problem, then? She put her niggling worry aside as

Brand spoke. "Don't tell me what I can and can't afford."

"I do your books, remember?"

"Sometimes I forget how much you know. Now, sit back and relax, will you?"

"Why are you doing this?"

"Can't a man treat the woman he loves to something special without her getting suspicious?"

"Yes, but—"

"Then enjoy!" His humor was infectious.

They toasted her trip and Carly talked about Diana and Barney, recalling some anecdotes from her friends' courtship.

Midway through dinner, Carly knew what was troubling Brand. It came to her in a flash of unexpected insight. She set her fork aside and lazily watched Brand for several moments.

"What's the matter?" He stopped eating. "Is something wrong with your steak?"

Carly shook her head. "No, everything's fine."

"Then why are you looking at me like that?" Brand watched her curiously as she stretched her hand across the table and took his.

"Running has been a problem ever since I met you, hasn't it?" she asked softly. "But, Brand, this time I'm coming back."

Brand nodded, still showing only a facade of unconcern. "I know that."

"But you were worried?" She released his hand.

He concentrated on slicing his rare steak, revealing little of his thoughts. "Perhaps a little."

"You don't need to worry. If I ever walk away, you'll know when and the reason why."

He answered her with a brief shake of his head, but Carly noticed that he was more relaxed now. "Do you want to go dancing after dinner?" he surprised her by asking.

"Dancing?" She eyed him suspiciously. He'd told her he didn't dance the first time they'd gone out for a meal. "I thought you said you didn't."

"That was before."

"Before what? Have you been taking lessons from Ginger Rogers secretly?" she teased lightly.

The humor drained from his eyes, and he sought and found her gaze. "No, that was before I ever thought I'd find anyone who'd make me want to dance again."

Chapter Seven

Carly eased the strap of her carry-on bag over her shoulder as she made the trek through the long jetway from the airplane into the main terminal at Sea-Tac Airport.

Her dark eyes scanned the crowd, finally catching a glimpse of Diana, who was nervously smoking a cigarette. Her friend hadn't changed. Not that Carly had expected her to. Somehow she never got used to the fact that Diana was only five foot four inches. Their hair color was the same ordinary shade of dark brown. But there the resemblance stopped. Carly was a natural sort of person who didn't bother much with fashionable hairstyles or trendy clothes. She was too proud of her individuality to be swayed by the choices

of others. But it was not so with Diana, who often
dressed in the most outrageous styles and clothes.
Flamboyant was an apt one-word description of Diana.

"Carly."

Carly watched as Diana put out her cigarette with
unnecessary vigor and marched through the crowd.

"Darling, you're gorgeous." Diana threw her arms
around Carly. Such an open display of affection was
typical of Diana, who acted as though she hadn't seen
Carly in years instead of only a few weeks. "But too
thin. You're not eating enough. I knew this would
happen. I've read about how hard it is to get supplies
into Alaska. You're starving and too proud to admit I
was right. I hope to God you're ready to move back
where you belong."

Carly laughed brightly. "If you think getting supplies is difficult, you should try heating an igloo."

They teased and joked as they took the escalator to
the baggage claim area, where Carly picked up her
luggage.

"Where's Barney?"

"Working. He sends his love, by the way." Each
carrying a suitcase, they crossed the sky bridge to the
parking garage. "Wait until you see his wedding gift
to me."

"Diamonds? Furs?"

"No," Diana shook her head solemnly. "I told him
not to bother. Neither one of my other husbands did."

When Diana paused in front of a red convertible,
Carly's mouth dropped open. "The car. Barney got

you a red convertible?'' This was the kind of car Diana had always dreamed of owning.

Diana shook her head in feigned dismay. "That's only half of it."

"You mean he got you two cars?"

One delicately outlined brow arched. "Better."

"Better?" Carly gasped playfully.

A few minutes later Carly understood. Diana exited off the freeway and took a long, winding road that led to an exclusive row of homes built along the shores of Lake Washington.

"Barney bought you a house!"

"He said I'd need some place to park the car," Diana explained excitedly as she pulled into the driveway and turned off the ignition. "I still get a lump in my throat every time I see it." She bit her bottom lip. "I remember not long after we met, Barney was telling me that someday he was going to build a house. I told him about the one I had pictured in my mind from the time I was a little girl. A house full of love."

"And Barney built you that house." Carly shook her head in wonder. "Tell me again where you found this man!" she begged theatrically.

"The crazy part of it is how much Barney loves me!" Diana sounded shocked that anyone could care for her with such fervor. "And it isn't like I'm a vestal virgin who's coming to him spotless. With my track record, any sane man wouldn't touch me with a ten-foot pole." Tears filled the dark brown eyes. "You know, Carly, for the first time in my life I'm doing something right."

Carly's hand squeezed her friend's as tears of shared happiness clouded her own vision. "Look at us," she said, half laughing, half sobbing. "You'd think we were going to a funeral. Now, are we going to sit out here all day or are you going to show me the castle?"

With a burst of energy, Diana led Carly from room to room, pointing out details that a casual inspector might have overlooked. Every aspect of the house was impressive, with high ceilings and the liberal use of polished oak.

"It's beautiful," Carly said with a sense of awe. "I counted four bedrooms."

"Two boys and a girl," Diana announced thoughtfully. "As quickly as we can have them."

Shaking her head, Carly eyed her friend suspiciously. "And you used to tell me diaper rash was catching."

Laughing, Diana led the way into the kitchen and opened the refrigerator. "Barney and I can hardly wait for me to get pregnant." She handed Carly a cold Pepsi. "Here, let me show you what I got him for a wedding gift." She led Carly into the family room off the kitchen and pointed to the leather recliner. "They delivered it a couple of days ago. For a while I was afraid it wouldn't arrive before the wedding."

"I'll bet Barney loves it."

"He hasn't seen it yet," Diana explained. "He won't be moving in until after the wedding."

"Oh." The surprise must have shown in Carly's eyes. The couple had been sleeping together for months.

"I suppose it sounds hypocritical at this point, but Barney and I haven't lived together since we talked to the pastor."

"Diana," Carly said softly. "I'm the last person in the world to judge you. Whatever you and Barney want is fine with me."

"I know. It's just that things are different now. We're different. We even started going to church. Every Sunday. At first I thought the congregation would snicker to see someone like me in church. But they didn't. Everyone was so warm and so welcoming. In fact, a few ladies from the women's group volunteered to have a small reception for us after the wedding."

"That's wonderful."

"Barney and I thought so, too." Diana's eyes lit up with a glow of happiness. "For a long time I expected something to happen that would ruin all of this. It's been like a dream, and for a time I felt I didn't deserve Barney or you or the people from the church."

"But, Diana—"

Diana interrupted by putting her hand over Carly's. "My thinking was all wrong. Pastor Wright pointed that out to me. And he's right. We did a lot of talking about my background, and now I see how everything in my life has led to this point."

Carly wondered if she'd ever find this kind of serenity or that special glow of inner happiness Diana had.

"I hope you're hungry," Diana said. "We're supposed to meet Barney in a half hour for lunch."

"I'm starved." Carly sighed dramatically. "As you've guessed, I haven't eaten a decent meal in weeks. Food's so hard to come by in the Alaskan wilderness. And I just haven't acquired a taste for moose and mountain goat."

Dressed in her pajamas, Carly sat cross-legged on top of Diana's huge king-size bed. "One thing I've got to do tomorrow is buy a dress. I couldn't find anything I liked in Anchorage, but then, I wasn't in much of a mood to shop."

"I already beat you to it. Knowing you'd put it off to the last minute, I scheduled time for us to go shopping tomorrow." Diana sat at the vanity, applying a thick layer of white moisturizing cream to her face. "Are you going to tell me about him or do I have to pry every detail out of you with the Chinese water torture?"

Carly dodged her request. "It may take months for you to get pregnant if Barney sees you smear that gook on your face every night."

"Quit trying to avoid the subject." Some of the teasing humor left Diana's eyes.

"All right, all right. I'm in love with Brand." The burst of happy surprise Carly had expected didn't follow.

"I already knew that. I've known from the moment you started writing to me about him. Obviously, he's in love with you, too."

Carly answered with a curt nod. "He asked me to marry him before I flew down here."

"And?"

"I told him no," Carly said sadly. "I can't, Diana. He's everything I want and everything I fear all rolled into one."

"Is it because of his wife and the two kids?"

"Aren't you nervous about the wedding?" Carly asked hastily, wanting to change the subject.

"This is my third wedding. I'm over the jitters. Now, let's get back to you and Brand."

"I don't want to talk about me," Carly said stubbornly. "Brand and I have gone over every detail until we're blue in the face. I can't change the way I feel."

"Sweetie." Diana only called her that when she was either very sad or very serious. "It's time you grew up."

Somehow she'd known that Diana, of all people, would understand. "All right, I admit that there will probably never be anyone I'll feel this strongly about again."

"But you're afraid?" Diana prompted.

"Out of my wits."

Diana's soft laugh filled the bedroom. "I never thought you'd admit it."

"This is the exception." Carly fiddled with the nylon strings of her pajama top. "In a lot of ways you and I are alike. For one thing, I have trouble believing Brand could honestly love me. I'm terribly insecure, often irrational, and a card-carrying emotional cripple."

"Do you remember how long it took Barney to convince me to marry him? Months."

"Brand's not as patient as Barney. He thinks that because we're in love everything will work itself out."

"He *sounds* like Barney," Diana murmured more to herself than for Carly's benefit.

"His children are coming to Alaska the middle of next month." Carly's voice was unsteady. Shawn and Sara were the focus of her anxieties.

"Sandra's children." Diana had a way of hitting the nail on the head.

Carly winced and nodded.

"And nothing's ever frightened you more."

"Nothing." Her whisper was raw with fear.

"All our lives I thought you were the fearless one," Diana whispered, "but deep down you've been as anxious as I have. Be happy, Carly." She wiped the moisturizer from her face with tissues as she spoke. "As much as I'd like to, I can't tell you what to do. But I urge you to stop being so afraid of finding contentment. Believe that Brand loves you. Count yourself blessed that he does."

Carly laughed, but the soft sound came out more like a sob. "For not wanting to tell me what to do, you sound like you're doing just that."

Diana's eyes locked with Carly's in the vanity mirror. "Go for it, kid."

Carly couldn't remember a more beautiful wedding. Tall white baskets filled with huge floral arrangements adorned the sanctuary. A white satin ribbon ran the length of the railing in front of the altar.

Barney, the short jeweler Diana had met at a Seahawk's football game, stood proudly with his bride at his side. His dark hair had thinned to a bald spot at the top of his head, and his nose was too thin for his round face. Barney definitely wasn't the type of man to stop female hearts. Carly recalled the first time she'd met him, and her surprise that Diana would be dating such a nondescript man. But her attitude had soon changed. From the first date, Barney had treated Diana like the most precious woman in the world. Carly loved him for that. Barney's love and acceptance had changed Diana until she glowed and blossomed under it.

Diana had never looked happier or more beautiful. She stood beside Barney, their fingers entwined, linking them for life. As the maid of honor, Carly held the small bouquet Diana had carried to the altar.

Both Diana's and Barney's voices rang strong and true as they repeated their vows. A tear of joy slipped from the corner of Carly's eye as Barney turned and slipped the gold wedding band onto Diana's slim finger.

Diana followed, slipping a simple gold band onto Barney's thick finger, her eyes shining into his as she did so. This time Diana was confident she was marrying the right man.

"I now pronounce you husband and wife." The pastor's strong voice echoed through the church.

Diana looked at Barney with eyes so full of love that Carly felt a lump in her throat. Whatever the future held, these two were determined to nurture their love and faith in one another. The commitment was on their faces and in their eyes for everyone to read. And it didn't go unnoticed.

The reception was held in the fellowship hall connected to the church. The wedding party was small. Diana had invited only a few friends, while Barney had asked his two brothers and their families. Three or four other couples who had met Diana and Barney through the church also attended.

Carly stood to the side of the reception hall and sipped her punch. Her eyes followed the newly married couple. Suddenly an intense longing she couldn't name filled her. She wanted Brand with her. She wanted to turn and smile at him the same way that Diana was smiling at Barney. And more than that, she needed to see again the love that had shone from his eyes as he had waved goodbye to her at the airport. Her chance for happiness was waiting for her in Anchorage; the question was whether or not she had enough courage to look past the fact that Brand had known this kind of love and happiness before meeting her.

Carly paused and took another sip of the sweet punch. With all her hang-ups, she wondered what kind of mother she would be to Shawn and Sara. Only a minute ago she'd begun to feel a little confident; now she was filled with as many insecurities as ever. As much as she wanted to find parallels in her relationship with Brand and Diana and Barney's, she couldn't. The two couples faced entirely different circumstances.

Following the reception, Diana, Barney, Barney's relatives and Carly went to dinner at Canlis', a plush downtown restaurant. From the restaurant, the new-lyweds were leaving for a two-day honeymoon in the San Juan Islands. Diana insisted that Carly stay at the house, giving her the keys to the car so that she could drive it home.

It was some time later when, yawning, Carly walked into the guest bedroom and kicked off her tight heels. The thick carpet was like a soft cushion under her bare feet. The day had been full and she was tired, but the thought of bed was dominated by her need to hear Brand's voice.

He answered on the first ring, and even the long-distance echo couldn't disguise how glad he was to hear from her.

"How was the wedding?"

"Wonderful. Oh, Brand, I can't even describe how beautiful everything was."

"Well, I certainly hope it had the desired effect. There's only one wedding I want to attend, and that's *ours*." The teasing inflection in his voice failed to mask a thread of seriousness that Carly couldn't ignore.

"Are we going to argue long distance?"

"Arguing is the last thing I have on my mind." His voice became low and sensual. "In fact, if you knew what I was thinking, you'd probably blush."

"I do not blush." She might be a virgin, but she wasn't a shrinking violet.

Brand chuckled. "This time you would."

"I take it you miss me."

"Dear God," he said and laughed. "You have no idea."

"But I've only been gone a day."

"Almost two days. Not that I've noticed."

"I can tell."

"Well, come on. Say it," Brand prompted.

"Say what?"

"How much you've missed me. I'm especially interested about what went on in that beautiful mind of yours when you heard your friend repeat her vows. Did you think of me and wish that I was at your side so we could say them to one another?"

"Obviously you crept into my thoughts or I wouldn't have phoned." Carly would admit to nothing. She wrapped a strand of hair around her ear. Sometimes Brand knew her as well as she knew herself.

"But you won't admit to thinking about me during the wedding ceremony."

"You're right," Carly said in a low, sensual tone. "I won't admit to anything until I see you."

She heard Brand's swift intake of oxygen. "You'd better not have changed your mind about flying home Sunday."

"No, I'll be there. But don't say anything to George—he thinks I'm arriving on Monday."

"Don't worry. My lips are sealed."

"Darn. I have a thing about sealed lips."

"What's that?"

"I never kiss them," she announced and the sound of Brand's laughter mingled with the sound of her own merriment.

They talked for almost an hour, and could have gone on for another. Even after she hung up, Carly itched to phone him back and say all the things she hadn't had the courage to tell him the first time. Only the thought of the phone bill and the knowledge that she would be back home Sunday evening deterred her.

After talking to Brand, Carly took a hot bath, soaking up the warmth of the water. A chill had found its way into her blood. Tomorrow she would be driving to Purdy and the State Correctional Center for Women. Jutta Hoverson hadn't replied to Carly's latest correspondence, but one thing was certain. It wasn't the charcoal sketches Carly was interested in seeing. It was Jutta Hoverson.

Visiting hours were scheduled for the afternoon, so Carly had a late breakfast and lingered over the morning paper. She dressed carefully, wanting to appear neither too casual nor too formal. Finally, she chose a three-piece slacks suit that was just right. Fleetingly, she wondered if Jutta had any apprehensions about the meeting. Probably not.

Once at the Center, Carly signed in at the desk and was asked to place her valuables in a rented locker. Carly had seen identical ones at airports and bus depots. She placed her purse inside, inserted the quarter and stuck the key into her jacket pocket.

The waiting area was soon filled to capacity. An uncomfortable sensation came over Carly as she studied the others in the room. Not in the habit of making snap judgments about people, Carly was amazed at her immediate distrust of the few men who regarded her steadily. Carly admitted that she did stick out like a little green Martian. Compared to the others, she was decidedly overdressed. Her uneasy feeling intensified as the waiting area emptied. The visitors were led away in small groups to another room, where they walked through a metal detector and were briefly questioned. From there, each group was directed into a large room with several chairs against the walls.

There Carly took a seat close to the window and tried to ignore the iron bars that obstructed the view. The oppressive silence of the room was interrupted by a crying child who was pitifully asking to see his mommy.

An iron door slid open and the women prisoners filed into the room one by one. Carly had filled out a card when she entered the building, requesting to see Jutta Hoverson, but she had no way of identifying her.

The little boy broke loose and ran into the arms of one woman, who swooped him into her embrace. The scene was a touching one and Carly wondered what the young woman had done in her life to be thus separated from her child.

"Are you Carly?"

Carly's attention skidded from the youngster to the tall, thin woman standing before her. "Yes." She rose. "Are you Jutta?" Never would Carly have envisioned Jutta this way. The child in the painting had given little clue to the woman's appearance. The hair, long and hanging in straight braids, was the same shade of brownish-red, except that it was mostly gray now. The glasses she wore slipped down the bridge of her nose and Carly doubted that they had ever fit her properly. Her clothes were regular street clothes, but drab and unstylish. Jutta looked as nervous as Carly felt.

"It's good to meet you," Carly began stiffly.

"They wouldn't let me bring out the sketches without some kind of approval beforehand."

"That's all right." The stilted, uncomfortable feeling intensified. "Can we sit down and visit for a while?"

Jutta shrugged one shoulder and sat. "I don't suppose you've got a cigarette?"

"Yes . . ." She turned to reach for her purse, then remembered what she'd done with it. "No, I'm sorry—they're in my locker."

"What did you do with the key?"

Carly pulled it from her jacket pocket and showed it to her.

"If you have a safety pin, put it on the inside of your lapel. That way no one will lift it off you."

"Oh." It hadn't occurred to Carly that anyone would. With shaking hands, she did as Jutta suggested.

"I suppose you're curious to know what I did to end up here," Jutta challenged, quickly putting Carly on the defensive.

The one thing Carly didn't want to do was make the woman uncomfortable. "Not unless you want to tell me."

"I don't see why not. It's a matter of public record. I forged checks, and it wasn't the first time, either."

"How long is your sentence?"

"Long enough. I've been in Purdy two years now and I don't expect to get approval from the parole board for another two."

"Did you start painting in . . . here?"

"Yes."

"I thought the painting of the child was excellent."

"I won't sell that one."

"Yes, I realize that," Carly assured her quickly. "Since it obviously means so much to you, I don't think you should."

"What I can't understand is why someone like you would want it." Jutta's deep blue eyes narrowed as they studied Carly. "You're a regular uptown girl."

That was probably the closest thing to a compliment that Jutta would give. "The picture reminded me of myself when I was five."

"You were poor?"

Carly answered by nodding her head.

"You seem to be doing all right now."

"Yes. I'm fine."

"You haven't mentioned a man. Are you married?"

"No." Carly shook her head automatically. "But . . . I've been thinking about it," she said stiffly.

"It seems to me if you have to think about it, then you probably..."

"No," Carly interrupted. "It isn't that. I love him very much. But...well, he's got children."

"I'd have thought you'd be the type to like children."

"I do." Carly was uncomfortable with this line of conversation and sought a means of changing it. "Do...do you have children?"

"I've got a kid, but I never married," Jutta stated defensively. "He's grown now. I haven't seen him in ten, maybe fifteen years. Last I heard he was in prison. Like mother, like son, I guess. Don't keep in contact with him much."

Carly hadn't expected Jutta to be so honest. If anything, she'd thought the artist would rather not answer personal questions. "I don't remember my mother," Carly admitted softly, her gaze falling to her hands. "The state took me away from her and put me in a foster home when I was five."

"Have you seen her since?"

"No. I did try to find her when I was twenty. But I didn't have any luck. To be honest, I think her drinking killed her."

"A lot of women get hooked on that stuff. And worse."

"I don't feel any bitterness or anything. I can hardly remember her."

"She beat you?" Jutta asked.

"No. At least I don't think so."

"Then you were lucky."

"Yes," Carly agreed. "I was lucky."

Carly thought about their conversation as she drove back toward Seattle over the Narrows Bridge. Jutta wasn't at all what she'd expected. The woman was forthright and sincere. She was brusque and a little abrasive, but her life had been hard, her experiences bitter. In some ways Carly saw the mother she had never known in Jutta. And in other ways she saw reflections of the proud child of the painting.

Their conversation had been stilted in the beginning, but by the end of the hour they were slightly more comfortable in one another's company. Jutta had explained far more about herself than Carly had thought she would. She said that there was a letter waiting for Carly in Anchorage and admitted, almost shyly, that she enjoyed getting mail.

Diana and Barney returned home early Sunday afternoon, both radiant.

"Welcome home," Carly said and embraced Diana warmly. "I didn't expect you back so soon."

"Barney's got a business meeting first thing Monday morning. And I wanted to get back early enough to beat the traffic."

"I've already called for a taxi." Carly glanced at her watch. "My flight leaves in another two hours."

"But I thought we'd have time to visit."

"Are you nuts?" Carly said and kissed her friend on the cheek. "I'm leaving so you and Barney can begin your married life in peace."

"We're going to be so happy," Diana said with confidence.

"I know you are. And I can't think of anyone who deserves it more than the two of you."

"I can." Diana's happy gaze clouded with concern. "I want you to know this kind of happiness, Carly. You're the closest thing I have to family. If you walk away from Brand, it's something you'll regret all your life."

Unable to break the melancholy air that suddenly seemed to hang between them, Carly hugged her friend again. "I'm not going to," she whispered.

The taxi arrived ten minutes later. Amid protests from both bride and groom, Carly left. Diana and Barney, arms entwined, stood on the sidewalk waving as the driver pulled away. From her position in the back seat, Carly turned and blew them both a kiss. Leaning the back of her head against the seat, Carly closed her eyes for the remainder of the ride to the airport.

Although he hadn't mentioned it, Carly was certain Brand would meet her plane. And when he did, that look would be in his eyes again—the look that demanded an answer. She wanted to marry him, but pushing all her doubts and insecurities aside wouldn't banish them.

Jutta had assumed that Carly couldn't love Brand if she hesitated before marrying him. Yet, just the opposite was true; every minute she discovered she loved him more. Little by little, bit by bit, he had worked his way into her life, until she realized now how lost she would be without him.

Diana had said the time had come for her to grow up, to set aside the hurts of her childhood and deal with the realities that faced her. How simple it sounded. But she was dealing with emotions now. Not reason. So many times in the last few days Carly had caught herself wondering about Brand and Sandra. Such thinking was dangerous. And unreasonable. Sandra was gone. *She* was here now, and crazy in love with the leftovers of Sandra's life.

The days were growing longer now, and when the plane touched down at the Anchorage airport the sun was still shining. As she'd hoped and as she'd feared, Brand was there. She paused midstride when she saw him standing to the side, waiting for her. He seemed tired, and his eyes were sad. She hadn't seen him like that since the night he'd first told her about Sandra.

When he smiled the look vanished, and her heart melted with the potency of it. Quickening her pace, she walked to his side. "Hi," she whispered, her eyes not leaving his.

"How was the flight?"

"Uneventful."

He took the carry-on bag from her grasp, his eyes not quite meeting hers. "All day I had the feeling you'd decide to stay in Seattle."

"I told you I was coming back."

He nodded as if he didn't quite believe her. "I don't know, Carly." He ran a hand through his thick hair in an agitated action. "I've told myself a thousand times

I was making a fool of myself. It's not a comfortable feeling to think the woman you love is going to walk out on you without a minute's hesitation.''

''Brand,'' she argued, ''I'm not going to do anything of the sort.''

Long strides took him to the area where they were to wait for her luggage. ''I don't like what I'm becoming...''

A chill came over her at the grim displeasure in his voice. Carly's hand gripped his forearm. ''Do I get a chance to say something or do I have to listen to your tirade first?''

''Go ahead,'' he answered, without looking at her.

She swallowed. ''I guess the simplest way of saying it is yes.''

''Yes what?''

''Yes, I want to be your wife.''

Chapter Eight

Brand straightened and turned toward her. She watched as his face mirrored his confusion. "What did you say?"

"You did ask me to marry you." For a fearful instant, her dark eyes blazed. "And, by heavens, you'd better not have changed your mind. Not after all the soul-searching I went through to reach a decision."

"I haven't changed my mind." An intense look darkened his eyes and a muscle worked along the side of his lean jaw as his gaze centered on her upturned face. He looked as if he couldn't quite believe her. "Let's get out of here." He jerked her suitcases from the carousel at the baggage claim area and ushered her out of the airport terminal.

Brand didn't say another word until they were inside her apartment. His eyes had narrowed with impatience and the line of his mouth was stern. "Now, would you care to repeat yourself?"

"That I'd marry you?"

An incredulous light brightened his features as the beginnings of a smile spread across his wary countenance. "You mean it."

"Of course I do." Carly smiled softly as she reached out and traced the outline of his lips with the tip of her index finger.

Brand shuddered violently at her tender gesture and pulled her into his arms. Crushed against him, Carly opened her mouth to his probing kiss, reveling in the urgency of his touch. Again and again his lips ravaged hers as if he couldn't get enough of her.

"I won't let you change your mind," he whispered against her temple. "Not now. Not ever."

Weak and trembling, Carly pressed light kisses on his eyelids, his cheek and his jaw. "I'm not going to back out. I only pray that we're doing the right thing."

"We are." His arms tightened around her slim waist. "I know it in my heart."

He kissed her again with a gentleness that stirred her heart. She *was* doing the right thing. Yes, she was afraid, and there were many fears yet to face, but Diana was right. If Carly walked away from Brand and his children she would be turning away from the best thing that had ever happened to her. The choice was clear—either marry Brand or lose him forever.

Brand inhaled deeply and took a step back. His hands settled on either side of her face as his eyes met hers. "We'll get the blood test tomorrow."

Carly nodded. "Fine."

"And be married by Friday."

Her lashes fluttered down. Everything was happening so fast. Clearly, Brand feared she'd have second thoughts. "Okay," she agreed, but her voice wobbled.

His warm breath fanned her face an instant before he covered her mouth with his. Carly dug her fingers into his shoulders, unaccustomed to the sensations that he was arousing within her. Her lovemaking experience was limited, but Brand wasn't aware of that.

He led her to the sofa and, sitting beside her, he fumbled with the buttons of her blouse. His gaze was centered on the gentle fall and rise of her breasts as she breathed. Slowly, he eased the silky-smooth shirt from her shoulders. When his hand closed over her breast, Carly felt her nipple harden in his palm and she closed her eyes. A low moan of pleasure slipped from her throat when he discarded her bra and removed his own shirt in hurried, abrupt motions. Carly watched him, her head spinning helplessly. She sighed as he brought her back into his embrace and her bare torso met his. A rush of sensual excitement stole her breath away at the feel of his abrasive chest against her softness.

"You feel like silk against me," he said with a groan. "So smooth and soft." His open hands slowly caressed her bare back as his mouth traveled over the scented hollow of her throat and made a gradual descent.

A whirlwind of new, exciting sensations attacked her at the touch of his tongue on her breast. The hot fire building within her was growing almost unbearable. She wound her arms around his neck and buried her face in his throat, kissing him there with a compulsion she couldn't define.

"Carly," he groaned.

She arched against him and felt his male hardness against her thigh. His need was as great as her own, and Carly gloried in the knowledge.

Brand kissed her with driving urgency, pressing her back so that she was lying flat on the sofa.

"Carly...dear God." He brushed the hair from her face, his eyes finding hers. His fingers were shaking as he framed her face with his hands. "If we don't stop now, we'll end up making love right here."

Something in his eyes gave him away. "Are you afraid?" she whispered. He'd told her once that he hadn't made love to a woman since Sandra.

He released her and the silence stretched until Carly raised herself up on one elbow to study him. He regarded her steadily and nodded. "It's been a long time."

His honesty had been painful for him, but Carly offered him a trembling smile and lovingly kissed his brow. "We've waited this long. We can wait until Friday."

His mouth teased the corner of hers as their breaths mingled. "I don't deserve you," he murmured, holding her close. "I'm no bargain."

Her soft laugh followed. "For that matter, neither am I."

Later, as Carly dressed for bed, she examined herself in the mirror and was shocked at how pale and waxen her features were. Dear Lord, she prayed she was doing the right thing in agreeing to marry Brand. She was afraid, too, more than he realized. His honesty that afternoon had been a measure of his love. He wouldn't lie to her, and Carly admired him all the more for that.

The following morning, Brand picked her up and they went together for their blood tests.

"I'd like to have a minister marry us," Carly announced after they'd climbed into the car once more. They hadn't discussed who would perform the ceremony. From the way Brand was rushing things, Carly had the impression that he wanted a justice of the peace to do the honors.

Brand's fingers captured hers as he smiled faintly. "I'd prefer that, too."

An inner glow of happiness touched her eyes. "Where to next?" she asked cheerfully.

Brand reached for the folded newspaper on the seat between them. "I thought we'd look for a house to rent."

The mention of a house was a forceful reminder that Shawn and Sara would be joining them in less than a month.

"Yes," she said and swallowed back the surge of panic that filled her. "We should do that."

Brand handed her the newspaper. "We'll need at least three bedrooms."

Carly nodded stiffly and read off a couple of the listings. "Do you want to check them out now?"

His eyes sought hers. "Sure. We have all day."

They found a rental that sounded perfect through a real estate broker. The picture showed a modern home with three bedrooms and a large yard. Another room off the kitchen could be used as an office for Brand.

"It's perfect, I know it. We don't even have to go see it." Carly watched Brand's eyes agree as he read over the details.

"There's a problem." The broker went on to explain that the house was badly in need of a thorough cleaning and paint job.

"It'll work out fine," Carly assured Brand later when they were back in the car. "We can do the painting at night after work. If we work hard enough, everything will be ready by the time Shawn and Sara arrive."

"Carly." One corner of his mouth lifted. "The first weeks after we're married, we're going to have enough to do without fixing up a house."

She snuggled closer to his side and playfully nibbled at his earlobe. "I thought soon-to-be-husbands were supposed to humor their soon-to-be-wives."

"I have a lot more in mind than humoring." His voice was husky with longing as he turned her into his arms.

Carly surrendered to his kiss, wondering if she would always feel this rush of excitement at Brand's touch. She couldn't imagine it ever being any different.

After lunch they stopped in and talked to George, who pumped Brand's hand in congratulation and frowned when he heard Carly would need Friday off, in addition to a few days over the Memorial Day weekend.

Later, when Brand dropped her off at her apartment and left to do some errands, Carly had to pinch herself. She could scarcely believe that in a matter of days she was going to be both a wife and a mother.

A hot cup of coffee and a cigarette helped soothe her nerves. Carly stared at the fiery tip of the cigarette and sighed just before grinding out the butt in the glass ashtray. The time had come for things to change. A lot of things. Scooting out of her chair, she walked over to the garbage can and threw away the remaining cigarettes.

"I've been meaning to quit anyway," Carly told Brand that night after dinner. "Consider it my wedding gift to you."

"Carly," Brand began and paused, regarding her seriously. "You're under enough stress now without adding to it."

"But I want to quit. I've been meaning to for a long time. Haven't you noticed that I started smoking a low-tar-and-nicotine brand? It was either quit or get a hernia trying to get something out of those.'' She tried to make light of it, her attitude flippant, but already her nerves were stretched taut. But she'd do it. Sheer determination would get her through this—just as it would get her through the wedding and meeting Brand's children. Sandra would never have desecrated her body with nicotine.

''Do you want to call Diana and Barney?'' Brand asked later that night.

''No. Not until after we're married. Otherwise Diana will insist on flying up here.''

''And that bothers you,'' Brand inserted coolly.

''No,'' she said, fighting to keep any tightness from her voice. But did it? She pushed the nagging thought away. ''Brand, she's barely been married a week. There will be plenty of time for you to meet her. If you don't object, I'd like to phone her after the ceremony.'' At any rate, Carly couldn't see interrupting her friend's honeymoon.

''Will she be surprised?''

Carly knew Diana's reaction would be closer to shock. ''Yes.'' She laid her head on Brand's shoulder. ''But there are advantages to being married only a week after my best friend,'' she said lightly. ''We'll be able to celebrate our anniversaries together.''

Brand's arm came up around her shoulders. ''We'll have lots of those, Carly.'' His warm breath mussed her hair. ''You've given me so much. Now it's time for me to return some of that. We'll be happy, won't we?''

She closed her eyes at the tenderness in his voice and responded with a gentle shake of her head because her throat felt thick with emotion.

No week had ever passed so quickly. Friday evening, with only a handful of people present, Carly Grieves became Brandon St. Clair's wife. A simple gold band adorned her ring finger. With so many expenses coming their way in the near future, Carly had decided against diamonds. Brand wore a gold band identical to hers.

Following the ceremony, Brand's eyes smiled into hers. His arm wrapped around her waist and held her close. "Hello, Mrs. St. Clair."

"Hello, Mr. St. Clair."

George, looking uncomfortable in a suit and tie, shook Brand's hand and slipped him an envelope. "Just to give you a start on things," he said gruffly.

"Aren't you going to kiss the bride?" Carly asked her boss with familiar affection.

George cleared his throat and looked to Brand for permission.

"Go ahead," Brand urged and squeezed Carly's waist.

Standing on the tips of her toes, she lightly brushed her lips against George's cheek.

The older man flushed with pleasure. "I suppose this means you're going to be wanting days off every week."

"No. Things should settle back to normal once we return from Oregon," Carly said, lowering her gaze.

They would be making a trip to Portland next week. She didn't mention that Brand's children would be coming in less than a month. The changes that would mean in her schedule hadn't been discussed.

"Are you ready to leave?" Brand asked.

"For our prehoneymoon?" Carly questioned eagerly. Brand had been busy all week on what he termed "their surprise weekend plans." Carly suspected they wouldn't be leaving Anchorage, since they both were due back at work on Monday morning. Brand was scheduled to fly into Dutch Harbor on the Aleutian Islands in the first week of June; he wanted Carly to fly with him, and on the return trip they'd stay at the lodge at Lake Iliamna. That was to be their official honeymoon. But this first weekend was a surprise Brand had planned especially for her.

His late-model Chevy was waiting for them in front of the church. Brand helped her inside and ran around to the front of the vehicle. "Are you ready for this?" he asked as he inserted the key in the ignition.

Carly tucked her arm in his and leaned her head quietly against his shoulder. "I've been ready for this all my life, Brandon St. Clair."

"Do you want to guess where we're going?"

"I haven't the foggiest idea. But it must be special, after all the time you've dedicated to it this week." She had only seen him one night after work.

"Still not smoking?"

"Not once," she said with undisguised pride. The week hadn't been easy, but the cravings weren't as strong now. Maybe that was the reason Brand had stayed away, knowing she would be a bear those first few days.

His hand patted hers. "I'm proud of you."

"I don't know why I ever started." She'd been smoking for several years. And although her reasons for picking up the habit were unclear, her reasons for quitting were well-defined.

Brand pulled up to the curb and parked the car. "Recognize this?"

"The rental house?" Wide brown eyes turned to Brand. "We got it?" Brand hadn't mentioned the house since that first day.

"Come and see." He jumped out of the car and walked around to the passenger side, lifting her into his arms. He closed the car door with his foot.

One step inside the house and Carly saw that the real estate agent hadn't underestimated the extent of the repairs that it required. The walls were badly in need of paint and the entire place required a thorough cleaning.

"Close your eyes," Brand instructed. "All this is to be blocked from your mind." He carried her through the living room and down a long hallway.

"Brand, for heaven's sake, let me down," Carly objected. "You'll hurt your back."

"Don't tell me you're going to be one of those wives who does nothing but complain."

Carly laughed, her mood happy. "All right, I won't tell you." Playfully, she nibbled on the lobe of his ear.

Brand's hold tightened as he leaned forward and opened the door that led to the master bedroom.

The teasing laughter faded as Carly looked at the room for the first time. The walls were freshly painted in a light shade of blue. The navy blue bedspread and drapes were made from identical floral patterns.

"Oh, Brand," Carly breathed with a sense of awe. No wonder she hadn't seen him all week. He'd obviously been working here every night.

"The bedroom set is my gift to you," Brand said tenderly as he lowered her feet to the plush carpet.

Running her hand along the polished surface of the oak dresser, Carly felt a surge of love that ran so deep it stole her breath. Finding the words to say what was in her heart would be impossible. Letting the spark of appreciation in her eyes speak for her, Carly looped her hands around Brand's neck and kissed him. "Thank you," she whispered. "You must have worked every night."

Brand arched her closer by pressing his hands into the small of her back. She could feel his smile against the crown of her head. "At least I was able to keep my hands off you all week. Maybe it's old-fashioned, but I wanted you to be my wife before we made love."

A soft sigh escaped her and Carly laid her head on his muscular chest, closing her eyes. She'd thought a lot about tonight; her feelings were mixed. She was eager and excited, but apprehensive. In some ways she wished their lovemaking had been spontaneous and in others she was pleased that they'd waited until after the ceremony.

A finger under her chin raised her mouth to Brand's. When he kissed her, all of her pent-up longings for him exploded in a series of deep, hungry explorations. His hand manipulated the zipper at the back of her dress and artfully slipped the garment down her arms until it fell at her feet. Carly stood before her husband wearing only her creamy silk camisole and nylons. His hands at her breasts were tantalizingly intimate through the flimsy material and her nipples became pebble hard, straining against his palm.

"Brand," she murmured breathlessly. "My suitcase is in the car. My silky nightgown's in there." She became lost again in one of his kisses.

"I want to get these things off you," Brand groaned, "not add another set."

"But I bought it especially for tonight."

Immediately, his mouth hardened in possession, claiming the trembling softness of hers. "Does it mean that much to you?"

Her hands crept upward, fingers sliding into the thick hair that grew at the base of his neck. "No. All I need is you."

The silk camisole had ridden up, and she could feel the roughness of his suit against her bare midriff. The buttons of his shirt left an imprint on her soft skin.

Brand's mouth worked sensuously over hers as Carly moved away just far enough to unfasten his buttons and slide his suit jacket and shirt from him. He helped as much as he could, his warm breath igniting her desire. Once free of the restricting clothing,

Brand lifted the camisole over her outstretched arms so that her bare breasts nuzzled his chest. Wave after wave of exquisite pleasure lapped against her as her fingers sought his face, marveling at the strength of his rugged features, sharpened now in his excitement.

"Carly." He ground out her name as he shifted his attention to the creamy curve of her neck and shoulder. Wordlessly he took a step in retreat and, jerking aside his belt, removed the remainder of his clothes. Carly slipped out of her things and walked into his loving embrace. Brand lifted her into his arms and carried her to the bed.

"I love you, Carly," he whispered.

"And I love you," she returned. Her eyes misted with the intensity of her feelings. "I'll make you a good wife, Brand," she vowed. "And I'll be a good mother."

Tenderly, he laid her on top of the bed and placed a hand on either side of her face, his eyes boring into hers. "I already know that," he said and pressed the full weight of his lean body onto hers. Carly's pulse raced hot and wild and she knew he was just as aroused as she. His skin was fiery to the touch as she ran her hands down his back and hips. The heat fused them together.

One muscled leg slid intimately between hers, and Carly realized that fulfillment was only seconds away. She arched against him as he entered her trembling body and gasped as she was enclosed in a velvet mist of sensations.

"Carly?" Brand's voice was filled with wonder and surprise. "Did I hurt you?"

"No," she said with a heartfelt sigh. "It's wonderful."

He smoothed the hair from her face. "It gets better," he promised and began to move languidly. His hands and mouth coaxed gasps of pleasure from her until she was spinning higher than the stars into a heaven that was filled with the brightest constellations.

Carly thrilled to the sound of her name repeated again and again with words of love as Brand was lost in his own mindless whirl of ecstasy.

He cried out and held her tightly, kissing her cheek and eyes until his breathing had returned to normal. "Why didn't you tell me you were a virgin?"

"I didn't know how," she whispered, relaxing in the crook of his arm. "It was beautiful. I had no idea it would be this good."

"You're not disappointed?"

Carly raised herself up on one elbow and kissed the corner of his mouth. "You're joking."

Chuckling, he brought her back into his embrace, his hand pressing her head to his chest. "It was wonderful for me, too, Carly."

"Can we do it again?"

"Again?" he asked. "You shameless hussy, I've barely recovered from the first time. Give me five minutes."

"That long?" Her mouth made a languorous foray over his chest and up past his shoulder until she located his mouth, teasing him with short, biting kisses. She centered her attention on one side of his mouth and worked across to the other.

Brand's fingers tightened as he rolled with her in his arms so that their positions were reversed. He kissed her deeply, urgently. They made love quickly; the explosive chemistry between them demanded as much.

Carly clung to him afterward, not wanting ever to let him go.

"Satisfied now?" he whispered against her ear.

She shook her head. "I don't think I'll ever be satisfied."

"Me either," he said, holding her tightly at his side.

The next thing Carly knew, Brand was kissing her awake. "Are you hungry?"

"No, sleepy," she said with a yawn. "What time is it?"

"Ten. We haven't eaten dinner yet and I'm starved."

Carly sat up and pulled the sheet over her bare breasts. She'd hardly eaten all day and recognized the ache in the pit of her stomach as hunger pangs.

Brand slipped out of bed and reached for his pants. "I packed us a picnic basket. Wait here and I'll get it."

A couple of minutes later, Brand returned, carrying Carly's suitcase and a basket with a bottle of champagne and two glasses resting on the top.

Carly slipped her white lace and silk gown over her head while Brand opened the champagne and poured them each a glass.

"To many years of happiness," Brand said as he touched his glass to hers.

"To us," Carly added, and she took a sip of the sparkling liquid. The champagne tickled her throat. Laughing, she held her glass out for more. "What's there to eat?"

After refilling her glass, Brand opened the basket and brought out a large jar of green olives, a thick bar of chocolate and some fried chicken.

Carly was so pleased she wanted to cry. "Oh, Brand, you're marvelous."

"I know what you like."

"You do?" she asked him seductively, locking her arms around his neck. "You may have to revise your list."

He pulled her into his embrace and nuzzled her neck. "Gladly," he whispered just before his mouth claimed hers.

The only time they left the bedroom over the next two days was to make a quick run to Carly's apartment for more food, where they called Diana and Barney.

Diana answered the phone. "Carly!" she exclaimed. "This is a surprise. How's everything?"

"Great. But I thought you should know that I took your advice."

"My advice?"

"Yup. Would you like to talk to my husband?"

"Carly, you idiot! Why didn't you let me know? Yes, yes, let me talk to Brand."

Carly handed the phone to Brand and let him introduce himself to her friend. Wrapping her arms around his waist, she laid her head on his chest and was able to listen in on their conversation.

"No fair giving away all my childhood secrets." Carly's voice was playfully indignant when she took back the receiver.

"I wasn't," Diana denied with a telltale laugh. "Well, not *everything*."

"I like being married," Carly admitted with a catch in her voice. "Why didn't you tell me how great it is?"

"That's the problem," Diana said quickly. "You've got to be married to the right man."

Carly couldn't imagine sharing her life with anyone but Brand. "I've found him."

"So have I," Diana murmured. "Be happy, Carly."

Diana sounded as though she was close to tears. "I will. You too."

When she replaced the receiver, Brand took her in his arms. "Shall we name our first daughter Diana?"

"Diana?" Carly feigned shock, and teased him lovingly. "I was thinking more along the lines of Brandy—after her father."

Groaning, Brand shook his head. "I think I'll pray for sons."

"Brand." She took his hand and batted her long lashes. "You want to try it in the shower here?"

"Are you crazy? You nearly drowned me the last time."

"Yes, but it was fun, wasn't it?"

"Carly." Brand brushed the hair from his forehead and sighed, attempting to hide a smile. "I'm too old for those kinds of tricks. I prefer a nice, soft mattress."

"But I'm sure we must have done something wrong. Everyone makes love in the shower. At least they always do in the books I read."

Brand rolled his eyes mockingly. "All right, if you insist." He pulled her into his embrace and kissed her until she was breathless and clinging. "This is my punishment for marrying a younger woman," he complained.

"No..." She giggled. "This is your punishment for marrying a virgin."

Monday arrived all too quickly. Brand dropped her off at the apartment so she could drive her car to work.

"Do you want to meet back here this evening or at the house?"

Brand appeared to mull the question over. "The house. I'll pick up something for dinner and we can start painting after we eat."

Carly dreaded the job. Every room in the house needed a fresh coat. She wanted to do Shawn's and Sara's bedrooms herself. It seemed like a little thing, but it would help her to assimilate the fact that she was going to be a mother to those two. Having come into a similar situation, Carly was determined to make them feel loved and welcome from the beginning.

Brand met her at the house with hamburgers and two thick chocolate malts.

They sat at their hastily purchased kitchen table and Carly handed her malt back to Brand.

"I thought you liked chocolate."

"I do, but I'm watching my weight."

He arched one brow questioningly. "You're almost too thin as it is."

"That's because you nearly starved me to death this weekend," she tossed back.

He stood and came around to her side of the table. "Is that a fact?" he asked as he took her in his arms.

Her hands slid over his chest as their eyes met and held. The look in his eyes trapped the oxygen in her lungs.

"Ever read anything about making love on the top of a table?" he asked her in a low, husky tone, his eyes sparkling with mischief.

"Mr. St. Clair, you shock me."

Brand straightened and began undoing the buttons of his shirt.

Surprised, Carly watched him with her mouth hanging open. "I thought you were teasing."

"Nope." He unbuckled his belt.

"What about dinner?"

"It can wait." He reached over and unfastened the buttons of her blouse.

Holding her breath, Carly reached around and unzipped her skirt. "I thought you wanted to paint."

"What I want should be evident."

The skirt fell to the floor, leaving her standing in her teddy and designer stockings.

Brand was devouring her with his eyes. She undid his pants and dropped them to the floor.

Slowly, his hands shaking slightly, Brand removed the remainder of her clothes until they were both naked. Then he scooped her up and carried her down the hall.

Their lovemaking was urgent, explosive, and they clung to one another afterward.

"I thought you wanted to do it on top of the table."

"The bedroom wasn't that far away."

She smiled and kissed the side of his neck. "Almost too far, as I recall."

"I don't think you fully understand yet what you do to me," he whispered.

Carly rolled onto her stomach and hooked one bare leg over his. "If we keep this up we won't be finished with the house till Christmas."

Brand wrapped his arms around her and breathed in deeply. "The thought of hiring painters is growing more appealing by the minute."

Chapter Nine

The clock radio clicked and immediately soft music floated into the sunlit bedroom.

"Morning." Brand pulled Carly close to his side and leisurely kissed her temple.

"Already?" she groaned. Her eyes refused to open as she snuggled deeper within Brand's embrace. He was warm and gentle and she felt too good to move.

"Do you want me to make coffee this morning?"

Dark brown eyes flew open and she struggled to a sitting position. "No, I'll do it." Pausing at the side of the bed, Carly raised her hands high above her head and yawned.

"Aren't you ever going to let me get up first?" Brand teased with loving eyes.

"Nope." She leaned over and lightly brushed her mouth over his.

Brand's arms snaked around her waist and he deepened the contact with hungry demand. "What time is it?" he growled in her ear.

"Late," she teased and kissed him back spiritedly. "Much too late for what you have in mind." Giggling, she escaped from his embrace and grabbed her light cotton housecoat from the end of the bed before heading for the kitchen. Mornings were her favorite part of the day. Waking up with Brand was the culmination of every dream she'd ever hoped would come to pass.

When the coffee had finished perking, she carried a cup in to Brand. He generally left for work an hour earlier than she needed to be at Alaska Freight, but they woke together and Carly dutifully cooked his breakfast and got him out the door. Then she turned her efforts to preparing for her own day.

Brand strolled into the kitchen as she was laying strips of bacon into a hot skillet. The fat sizzled and filled the room with the aroma of cooking meat. Nuzzling the side of her neck, Brand wrapped his arms around her from behind and pressed his open palm against the fullness of her breast. "You smell good."

"That's not me, silly. That's the bacon."

His hand slid from her ripe breast and pressed against her smooth, flat abdomen. "We haven't talked about this much, but I'd like it if you got pregnant soon." He was so pensive and serious, a mood neither of them had had time for during these past few days.

Carly set down her fork and turned in his arms. "There's no rush, is there? I'd like to adjust to one family before starting another."

Brand pulled out a kitchen chair and sat down. His hands hugged the coffee mug. "There won't be two families, Carly, only one."

Sighing, she came up behind him and slipped her arms around his neck. "That's not what I meant. Even if I was to get pregnant tomorrow, there'd still be six years between that baby and Sara. It would be almost like raising two families."

Brand nodded and placed his hand on hers. "I know. It's just that I've been separated from Shawn and Sara for so long that I don't want to put any more distance between us. I want us all to be one family, no matter how many children you and I may have."

"We will," she promised and returned to the stove. This weekend was the time they'd arranged to fly to Portland so Carly could meet the children and Brand's mother.

The two eggs were overcooked when she set the plate in front of Brand. He didn't say anything, but she knew he preferred his eggs sunny-side up. "Sorry about that," she said a little defensively.

"Don't worry, they're fine."

Carly took a long swallow of her orange juice.

"Are you worried about this weekend?" Brand wanted to know.

She was terrified, but didn't want Brand to guess. "I'm looking forward to meeting your family...*our* family," she corrected.

Brand kissed her tenderly before heading out the door. "Have a good day, honey."

The endearment rolled easily off his tongue, and again Carly had the feeling it was the same affectionate term he'd used with Sandra. She cringed. The pain was quick and sharp. She bit the tender flesh inside her cheek as she pulled open a kitchen drawer and brought out a cookbook. For the sixth time in as many days, she read the recipe for chicken and dumplings. The meal was to be a surprise for Brand. Her first home-cooked dinner for her husband. Before very long, cooking would be a part of her everyday life, and the sooner she mastered the skill, the better. Shawn and Sara wouldn't be satisfied with green olives and chocolate. At least not after the first week.

The chicken was simmering on the stove as Carly dressed for work. The aroma of the bacon had made her feel weak with hunger. The small glass of orange juice had constituted her entire breakfast, and dumplings were out. To be on the safe side, she stepped on the scale. Two pounds. She'd been starving herself for ten miserable days and was only down two pounds. *Some* women were naturally svelte and others had to work at it. There wasn't any justice left in the world anymore, she grumbled on her way out the front door.

On her lunch break, Carly savored an apple, cutting it into thirty pieces. To take her mind off her need for a cigarette and how hungry she was, Carly drove into town and bought Sara a blue Smurf doll, and Shawn a book on Mount McKinley. She knew so little about these two who were destined to be a major part of her life. Her nerves were crying out with vague apprehension at the coming meeting. Fleetingly, she wondered how they felt about meeting *her*.

Before returning to the office, Carly stopped off at the apartment and checked on the dinner. She reread the cookbook instructions, confident that she had done everything properly. On the way out she stopped at the mailbox and collected the mail. Another letter from Jutta had arrived, and she ripped it open eagerly. Jutta sent her congratulations and claimed to be working on another oil painting that she thought Carly would like. She said she'd sell this one cheap.

Carly smiled, folded the letter and placed it back inside the envelope. Jutta seemed to think the only interest Carly had in her was because of her artwork. As their friendship grew, she was certain that Jutta would feel differently.

Because she wanted Brand to be pleasantly surprised with her dinner, Carly left the office early. George was being a dear about everything, including the extra days off over the Memorial Day weekend. Carly felt like giving him a peck on the cheek as she rushed out the door, but hesitated, knowing he wouldn't know how to react to her display of affection.

Brand got home a half hour after she did. "I'm home," he called cheerfully.

"Hi." She stepped from the kitchen. The corners of her mouth quivered with the effort to hold back her tears.

He stopped in the middle of the living room and sniffed the air. "Something smells bad."

"I know." She swallowed tightly. "I tried to cook something. It...it didn't work out." She gestured with one hand in angry bewilderment. "I...I don't know what I did wrong."

"Let me see," Brand offered as he headed for the kitchen.

"No!" she cried theatrically. "Don't go in there!"

"Carly." He gave her a look she felt he must reserve for misbehaving children.

Bristling, she cradled her stomach with her arms and shouted at him, "Go ahead then, have a good laugh."

Brand's eyes softened. "I'm not going to laugh at you."

"Why not? It's hilarious. How many husbands do you know who come home to be greeted with the news that their dinner's on the ceiling?"

Brand did a poor job of disguising his amusement.

Anger swelled like a flood tide in Carly until she wanted to scream. "I'm sorry I can't be as perfect as Sandra. I tried." Sobs took control of her voice. "I really tried."

"Carly. Dear God." He went pale and reached for her.

She broke from his grasp and gave way to huge hiccuping sobs, warding him off with her arm. "Don't you dare touch me.'' Each word was shouted and enunciated clearly.

Brand looked as if she'd struck him physically. He moved to the sofa and sat down. "I wondered." His voice was husky and raw. "But I didn't want to believe what was right in front of me."

The tears welled up and spilled down her face as she held her breath in a futile effort to stop the soft sobs.

"You gave up the cigarettes because of Sandra," Brand said flatly.

"She didn't smoke. I doubt that she ever did." Carly shouted angrily.

"And this insane dieting is because of her as well." Again it was a hard statement of fact and not a question.

"She was svelte."

"She was *gaunt*. Cancer does that to people." He rubbed his hand over his face. He was angry and didn't bother to conceal it. His mouth was pinched, his eyes hard and piercing. "What do I have to do to make you understand that I don't want another Sandra?"

"I thought..."

"I know what you thought." He vaulted to his feet and paced the floor. "For two years I grieved for Sandra. The ache inside me was so bad I ran from my children and separated myself from the world."

She kept her face averted, burying her chin in her shoulder. A dark curtain of hair fell forward.

"I love you, Carly. Your love has given me back my children and a reason to go on with my life. I don't

want to bury myself in the past again. With you at my
side, I want to look ahead at the good life we can
share." He turned and walked over to her. "I want
you. None other." Holding her, he wove his fingers in
her hair and forced her to look up at him. She couldn't
bear it and closed her eyes. Fresh tears squeezed their
way through her lashes. Every breath was a sob.

"What I feel for you is entirely different from my
love for Sandra," he continued. "She was an only
child, pampered and loved all her life. Even as a little
girl she was sickly. Her family protected her, and when
we married I took over that role."

Carly made an effort to strain away from the iron
clasp of his hands, but her attempt was futile as he
held her fast. She didn't want to hear any more about
Brand's first wife. Every word was like a knife piercing her heart.

"With Sandra, I felt protective and gentle," he said
in a low, soothing voice. "But with you I'm challenged and inspired. My love for you is deeper than
anything I'd ever hoped to find on this earth. Don't
compete with a dead woman, Carly."

She groaned with the knowledge that he was right.
There was no winning if she set herself up as a replacement for Sandra. Trying desperately to stop crying, she put her arms around his neck. "I'm sorry,"
she wept. "So sorry."

"I am too, love," he breathed against her hair. "I
should have recognized what was happening."

"I wanted to be perfect for you and the children."

"You are," he whispered tenderly. "Now, let's see what can be salvaged from your dinner."

"Not much, I'm afraid." She inhaled a steadying breath. "It may be far worse than you realize," she said, avoiding his eyes. "I think my dumplings may have dented the ceiling and we'll be out the damage deposit."

He started laughing then, with uncontrollable waves of mirth that were smothered only long enough to kiss her. Soon she was laughing with him, free and content with the knowledge that she was loved for herself.

Chapter Ten

Carly's fingers tightened around Brand's arm. "Are you sure I look okay?"

"You're beautiful." He squeezed her hand. "Perfect. They're going to love you."

Carly wished she had the same unfailing optimism. Shawn and Sara would be meeting them at the Portland Airport and the FASTEN YOUR SEAT BELT sign was already flashing in preparation for landing.

A thin film of nervous perspiration broke out across her upper lip and forehead and she wiped it away with her free hand. A thousand nagging apprehensions crowded their way into her troubled mind. The tightening sensation that attacked the pit of her stomach was identical to the one she'd experienced as a child whenever she'd been transferred into a new foster home. If she couldn't fit in with this new family, her life would be hell. The identical situation was facing her with Shawn and Sara. So much of her happiness with Brand depended on what would happen this weekend.

"Carly." Brand squeezed her hand again. "Relax. You're as stiff as new cardboard."

"I can't help it." Even her whisper was tortured. "What will we do if Shawn and Sara don't like me?"

"But they're going to love you," Brand argued.

"How can you be so sure?" She knew she sounded like a frightened little girl. How could anyone who'd leaped headlong into as many adventures as she had be so terrified of two small children?

Brand tightened his hold on her fingers and raised them to his mouth to tenderly kiss the inside of her palm. "They're going to love you because I do."

A flood of emotion clouded her eyes. "I want to make this work, Brand," she said, and she lowered her eyes so he couldn't see how maudlin she was becoming. "I really do."

"I know, love."

Carly's heart fell to her ankles when the plane touched down. A few minutes later, they were walking down the jetway that led to the cavernous terminal.

"Daddy, Daddy." The high, squeaky voice of a young girl came at them the moment they cleared the jetway.

Brand fell to one knee as blond-haired Sara threw herself into his arms. Shawn followed, and squeezed his father's neck so tightly Carly was amazed that Brand was still breathing. With a child on each hip, Brand stood.

"Shawn and Sara, this is Carly."

"Hi, Carly." They spoke together and lowered their eyes shyly.

"Hello."

"Daddy told us all about you," Sara said eagerly.

"Did you really climb a whole mountain?" Shawn queried with a hint of disbelief.

"It was the hardest thing I ever did in my life," Carly confirmed. "By the time I made it down, my nose was redder than Rudolf the Red-Nosed Reindeer's and my lips had blisters all over them."

"Wow." Shawn's big blue eyes were filled with awe. "I'd like to climb a mountain, too."

"Someday, son," Brand promised.

"Welcome home, Brand." A crisp, clear voice spoke from behind them.

Carly's attention was diverted to the older woman who stood apart from the small group. Her hair was completely gray, but her eyes were like Brand's—only faded and with a tired, faraway look.

Brand lowered the children to the floor. "Mother, this is my wife, Carly."

"Hello, Mrs. St. Clair." Carly stepped forward and extended her hand.

Brand's mother shook it politely and offered her an uncertain smile. "Please, call me Kay. With two Mrs.

St. Clairs around, there's bound to be some confusion."

Carly's spirits plummeted. Brand's mother didn't bother to disguise her lack of welcome. "Thank you," she said stiffly.

The older woman's eyes centered on the children, and softened. "Say hello to your new mother, children."

"Hello," they cried in unison, with eager smiles.

"I imagine you're tired," Kay St. Clair said conversationally on the way to pick up their luggage. "How was the flight?"

"Fine." Her mind searched frantically for something to say. "The weather certainly is nice." Bright, sunny skies had welcomed them to Oregon.

"But then, this must be paradise compared to Alaska," Kay returned stiffly.

The sky had been just as blue and beautiful in Anchorage, but Carly let the subject drop. There wasn't any reason to start off this relationship with an argument by comparing the two states. Indeed, Oregon was beautiful, but Alaska was equally so, in a different way. But Carly doubted that she could explain that to Brand's mother.

Lunch was waiting for them back at a stylish, two-story brick house with a meticulously kept yard and spotless interior. The entire house was so clean that Carly thought it had probably been sterilized. Framed pictures lined the fireplace mantel in the living room. There were photographs of Brand's two younger brothers and their families—and a picture of Brand

with Sandra on their wedding day. Carly's gaze was
riveted to the picture and the color washed from her
face. Abruptly, she turned away, unable to bear the
sight. By keeping the photo on the mantel, Brand's
mother had made her statement regarding Carly.

If Brand noticed how little she ate, he said nothing.
Shawn and Sara carried the conversation beautifully.
Their joy at seeing their father again was unabash-
edly enthusiastic. Carly discovered that it would be
easy to love those two, and she silently prayed that
they could come to love and accept her.

Kay St. Clair cleared her throat before addressing
Carly. "Tell me, what did your family think of this
rushed marriage?"

"My family?" Carly knew just by looking at Kay
St. Clair that she was a woman who put a lot of stock
in one's background. "I'm afraid I don't have any,
Mrs. St. Clair... Kay," she amended.

"Don't be silly, child, of course you do. Everyone
has family."

"Carly was raised in foster homes, Mother," Brand
explained for her.

"You were orphaned?" Kay St. Clair disregarded
her son and centered her full attention on Carly.

"Not exactly. I... I was taken from my mother by
the state when I was Sara's age."

"What about your father?" Shock had whitened
the aging face. Lines of displeasure wrinkled her brow
as Kay St. Clair set her fork aside.

"I never knew my father."

A soft snicker followed. "Are you sure your parents were married?"

"Mother," Brand barked angrily. "You're insulting my wife."

Carly placed a hand on his forearm and shook her head. She didn't want to cause any discord between Brand and his mother. "As a matter of fact, I'm not completely sure that they were."

Shawn and Sara had lowered their heads at the sound of raised, angry voices. They sat across from Carly looking so small and frightened that her heart ached with the need to reassure them.

"I hope you like surprises." Carly directed her words to the children. "Because I brought you each one."

"You did?" Shawn's face brightened with excitement. "Can I see it?"

"Can I see mine, too?" Sara's eyes found her grandmother's and some of her eagerness faded. "Please," she added politely.

"After we finish lunch," Carly promised and winked.

"Both Shawn and Sara have to brush their teeth first," Kay St. Clair inserted with a heavy note of censure.

"We never brush our teeth after lunch. Why do we have to do it today?" Shawn asked, a puzzled look in his eyes.

Their grandmother bristled noticeably. "Because we were too busy this morning. And until you move in with your father and . . . Carly, you must do as I say."

"Yes, Grandma," Shawn and Sara returned like finely trained puppets.

Carly watched as a frown worked its way across Brand's face. His mother's reaction to Carly seemed to be as much of a surprise to him as it was to her. Brand hadn't told her a lot about his mother, and she'd pictured her as the round, grandmotherly sort. Kay St. Clair wasn't that. She obviously cared for Shawn and Sara, and they returned that love, but she wasn't the warm, open person Carly had expected. But then, *she* wasn't the bride Kay St. Clair had anticipated, either.

"You have a lovely home, Kay." Carly tried again, knowing how difficult this meeting was for the older woman.

"Thank you. I do my best." The words were stiff and polite.

Carly swallowed tightly and looked at Brand. He was pensive, sad. He must have felt her gaze because he turned to her and gave her a reassuring smile. But it didn't fool Carly. She knew what he was thinking.

"Are there parks in Anchorage?" Shawn wanted to know.

"Lots of them," Brand confirmed.

"Are there any close to where we're going to live?"

"Not real close," Carly answered. "Farther than walking distance. But there's a big backyard with the house we're renting and I think we can probably persuade your dad to put up a swing set."

"Really?" Sara's blue eyes became round as saucers. "Grandma doesn't like us to play on her lawn."

"Children ruin the grass," Kay announced in starched tones. "So I take Shawn and Sara to the park."

"Almost every day," Sara added.

"How nice of your grandma to do that for you." Brand's mother had obviously tried hard to give the children a good home.

"I'll be sending a list of instructions with Shawn and Sara in June," Kay said, her eyes avoiding Carly's. "It's quite extensive, but I feel the transition from Oregon to Alaska will be much smoother for them if you follow my advice."

"Mother, I don't think—"

"That was thoughtful of you," Carly said, interrupting her husband. "I'll be pleased to look them over. Mothering is new to me, and I'll admit I have lots to learn."

"I'm finished now, Grandma," Shawn said eagerly. "Can I go brush my teeth?"

"Say it properly," Kay St. Clair ordered.

"May I be excused, please?"

A small smile of pride cracked the tight lines of the older woman's face. "Yes, you may be excused. Very good, Shawn."

"May I be expused, too?" Sara requested.

"Excused," Kay corrected. "Say it again."

"Excu . . . excused." Sara beamed proudly at having managed the difficult word.

"Yes. Both of you brush your teeth and then you can see what your father brought you."

"Carly brought the gifts." Brand corrected the intended slight.

Her meal was still practically untouched when Carly set her fork aside. "If you'll excuse me, I'll get the gifts from my suitcase." She didn't wait for Kay's permission, although she had the suspicion that it was expected of her.

The edge of the mattress sank with her weight as Carly covered her face with both hands. This meeting with Kay St. Clair was so much worse than she'd anticipated.

"We brushed our teeth." Shawn and Sara stood in the open doorway, startling her.

Carly forced herself to smile. "Then I bet you're ready for your presents."

They both nodded with wide-eyed eagerness.

Carly took out the two gaily wrapped packages from inside her suitcase and handed them to Shawn and Sara.

They sank to the floor and ripped off the ribbon and paper with a speed that was amazing.

"A Smurf dolly," Sara cried, her young voice filled with happy delight. "I've always, always wanted one." Two young arms circled Carly's neck and hugged her close.

Carly squeezed her fondly in return. "I'm glad you like it."

"Wow." Shawn's eyes were wide as he leafed through the picture book about the Alaskan mountains. "Thank you."

"Can we show Grandma?" Sara wanted to know.

"Of course." Carly followed them into the living room and noted again the disapproval in Kay St. Clair's eyes as she examined the gifts.

"I never did approve of those cartoons. They ruin a child's mind." She spoke to her son, but the slight was meant for Carly.

Indecision flared in Brand's eyes. He was as confused and unsure as Carly.

"Daddy said you were going to be our new mother. Can I call you Mom?" Sara asked, tugging at Carly's pants leg.

"If you like."

Discontent narrowed Kay St. Clair's mouth.

"Maybe you should call me Carly," she added hurriedly.

Brand brought Sara onto his knee. "You do what's the most comfortable for you."

"But I thought we already had a mom."

"You did," Kay St. Clair inserted coolly. "But she died."

"I think I'll call you Carly," Shawn stated thoughtfully after a long pause.

"If that's what makes you most comfortable." Carly responded as best she could under the circumstances. In one foster home where she'd lived, the parents had insisted she call them Mother and Father. Half the time the words had stuck in her throat. She wouldn't be offended if Shawn chose to call her by her first name.

"I think I'll call you Mom," Sara said from her father's knee. "I don't remember my other mommy."

"Sure you do, Sara," Kay St. Clair said sharply.

"All I can remember is that she smelled funny and she didn't have any hair."

A pained look flickered in Brand's eyes, one so fleeting that for a moment Carly thought she'd imagined it. But when he spoke, the pain in his voice confirmed the sadness in his eyes.

"That was the smell of the hospital and all her medicine," Brand explained carefully. "She lost her hair because the doctors were doing everything they could to make her well again. One of those treatments was called chemotherapy."

"And it made all her hair come out?" Two pairs of serious blue eyes studied Brand.

He nodded. "But your mother had real pretty hair. Just like yours, Sara."

The small face wrinkled in deep thought. "I wish I could remember her better."

"I do too, sweetheart," Brand murmured tenderly, holding his daughter in his arms.

Standing outside the circle of this poignant family group, Carly felt a brooding sense of distance, of separation. These three—four, if she included Brand's mother—were a family in themselves. The breath caught in her lungs as she watched them. All the emotional insecurities of her childhood suddenly reared up, haunting her, confronting her with the unpleasant realities of this marriage.

Again, just as she had been as a child, she was on the outside looking in. She belonged, and yet she didn't. She wasn't part of the family, but separate.

Any love and attention she'd received when growing up had always been what was left over from that given to the family's real children. She wasn't Brand's first wife, but his second. And a poor second, judging from his mother's reaction.

"If you'll excuse me, I'd like to lie down." Her voice was barely above a whisper. She avoided Brand's eyes as she turned toward the bedroom.

Her heart was pounding so hard and fast by the time she reached the bed that she all but fell onto the soft mattress. Everything she'd dreaded and feared was happening. And the worst part of it was that she could do nothing to change what was going on around her.

When she heard Brand's footsteps, Carly closed her eyes and pretended to be asleep. He hesitated in the doorway—before turning away.

Carly didn't know how long she stared at the ceiling. The muted sounds coming from the bedroom next to hers distracted her troubled thoughts. As much as she wanted to hide, Carly knew she couldn't stay in the bedroom for the entire weekend.

After combing her hair, she added blush to her cheeks. If she didn't, Brand was sure to comment on how pale she looked.

As she walked past Sara's room, Carly paused and glanced inside. The little girl was sitting on top of her mattress. A jewelry box was open in front of her and whatever was inside commanded her complete attention.

"Hi."

"Hi...Mom." Sara looked up and spoke with a shy smile.

"What are you looking at?"

"Pictures of my other mommy."

Carly's heart plummeted. She was a fool to believe that Sandra wouldn't haunt her. Borrowed dreams were all the future held. Another woman's husband. Another woman's children.

"Would you like to see?"

Some perverse curiosity demanded that Carly look. Sitting on the bed beside the sweet, blond-haired child, she examined each color print.

"My hair is like hers, isn't it?"

"Yes." The strangled sound that came from Carly's throat made Sara turn and stare at her.

"She was real pretty, too," Shawn said from the hallway. "Sometimes she sprayed on perfume and smelled good." Shawn seemed to want to correct his sister's memory.

"Did she read to us?" Sara inquired softly. "Like Grandma does sometimes?"

"Yup. Don't you remember, Sara? Don't you remember anything?"

Carly couldn't stand much more of this. She was certain the children didn't often talk about their mother. Brand's presence had resurrected these curious memories. The pain it caused her to listen to them speak about Sandra was beyond description. She couldn't take their mother away from them, but she wasn't sure that she could live in the shadow of Sandra's memory.

"I think I'll go find your father," Carly said, hiding behind a cheerful facade.

"He's talking to Grandma on the patio," Shawn provided. "We're supposed to be resting." He added that second fact with a hint of indignation. "Second-graders shouldn't have to take naps," he mumbled under his breath just loud enough for Carly to hear. "When we come and live with you and Dad, I won't have to, will I?"

Carly ruffled the top of his blond head. "No," she whispered. "But don't say anything to your grandmother."

Shawn's wide eyes sparkled and he shared a conspiratorial smile with Carly.

"When are we moving to Anchor...Alaska?" Sara asked, tucking the pictures back inside the jewelry box.

"Three weeks." Hardly any time at all, Carly realized. Certainly not enough to settle the horrible doubts she was facing.

"Will you read to us and tell us stories?"

Carly stared blankly at the pair. "If you like."

"Goody." Sara clapped her hands gleefully.

"Shh," Shawn warned. "Grandma will hear."

Raised voices on the patio outside halted Carly halfway through the kitchen. Brand and his mother were having a heated exchange. Their voices struggled to remain calm and composed. Carly doubted that Brand's mother had ever shouted.

"But you hardly know her," Kay returned with an uncharacteristic quiver that revealed how upset she was.

"I know everything that's necessary. Carly's given me back a life I thought I'd lost when Sandra died." There was an exasperated appeal in the way Brand spoke.

"There was no need to remarry so soon. Certainly you could have found someone more suitable," Kay St. Clair said as she examined the rose bushes that grew in abundance around the patio.

Carly stood next to the sliding glass door, but neither was aware of her presence.

"I wish you'd give her a chance, Mother. Carly's the best thing that's ever happened to me. Don't I deserve a little happiness? Shawn and Sara . . ."

"That brings up another matter," his mother interrupted crisply. "How can you possibly think Carly is a proper replacement for the care I've given Shawn and Sara? When I told you I wanted to relax and travel for a time, I assumed you'd hire a housekeeper. I had no idea you'd marry the first woman to turn you on."

Brand's jaw went white. Frustration drove deep grooves into his face as he struggled to restrain his anger. The lines that were etched out from his eyes relayed the effort it took. There was a silent, dangerous glare in his eyes. "Carly is everything I've ever hoped to find in a woman."

Slowly, deliberately, Brand's mother shook her head with disapproval. "Can't you see that she's trying to bribe the children? Bringing them presents, telling them about a swing set. Really, Brand. And her family..."

"What does that have to do with anything?" Brand's tight expression was disbelieving and grim.

"Honestly, son, sometimes you can be so blind." Kay cut a delicate rosebud from the flowering bush. "I don't mean to sound crass when I say that Carly is hardly the type of woman that men marry."

Shock waves tumbled through Carly. Her hand reached for the kitchen counter to steady herself. Her knees felt so weak that she thought for a moment that she might collapse. In all her life no one had ever said anything that could hurt her more. With an attitude that bordered on the fanatical, she'd tried desperately not to be anything like her mother. Anger and outrage seared her mind.

Brand looked as if he was about to explode.

Stepping onto the patio, Carly tilted her head at a proud angle. "You will apologize for that comment, Mrs. St. Clair."

Carly didn't know who was more shocked: Brand or his mother.

Kay was obviously flustered, but to her credit, recovered quickly and cleared her throat. "It's often been said that people who listen in on conversations don't hear good things about themselves."

Brand moved to Carly's side and slipped an arm around her waist, bringing her close to him. "You owe us both an apology, Mother."

Carly didn't want him to touch her but hadn't the strength to escape him. She felt stiff and brittle. Her heart was pounding so loudly, she was convinced the whole city could hear it.

Kay St. Clair conceded. "Perhaps. Only time will prove what I say. Until then, I can only offer my regrets for any thoughtlessness on my part." Without a hint of remorse, she returned her attention to the roses.

Brand took Carly's hand and pulled her into the kitchen. "Let's get out of here," he said with grim anger. "I won't have you subjected to this."

"No." Her throat worked convulsively. "We can't."

"Like hell." He raked a hand through his hair, his voice tight with impatient anger. "You don't have to take this from anyone. Least of all my mother."

Gently, Carly shook her head. "She loves you, and she loves Shawn and Sara. I'm a stranger who's invaded her world. And I'm not carrying the proper credentials."

"Carly." Brand frowned, unsure.

"I understand her better than you think," Carly said, her hurt and outrage checked. "If we leave now, the situation will be unbearable for Shawn and Sara."

"We could take them with us," Brand argued.

"And cause an even greater rift between you and your mother? Taking the children now would be heartless. She loves them, Brand."

"But she's hurt you and I won't stand for that." His eyes roved over her face intently.

"Your mother's doubts and mistrusts are natural."

Brand's fingers bit into the tender flesh of her upper arm. "Don't make excuses for her."

Carly closed her eyes and slowly shook her head. "The family I moved in with when I was fourteen had a natural daughter the same age. She hated me. It wasn't that I'd done anything. But I was there. I took away from the attention and love she felt was *her* due—not mine. I was a stranger with a murky past."

Brand brought her into his arms. "You're not a teenager anymore, Carly. You can't compare that to what's happening with my mother now."

Her smile was sad. She wouldn't argue with him, but in her heart, she knew. The situation was no different—and in many ways it was worse.

Carly lay awake that night. She could tell by the way Brand was breathing that he wasn't asleep either. The space between them seemed greater than just a few inches. In some ways whole universes stretched between them.

"You awake?" he whispered.

"Yes." She turned to cuddle him, nestling her head against his shoulder. The need to feel his arms around her was paramount. "I'm cold."

Immediately, Brand's arms brought her more fully into his embrace. "Tell me what happened in that foster home you were talking about earlier."

"Why?"

"I need to know," he returned in a slow, uneven murmur.

"Her name was Joyce," Carly murmured softly. "She never did learn to like me. I was a threat to her. Not with just her family, but at school as well. When we were allowed to date, it didn't matter who asked me

out, Joyce had to prove that she could take that boy
away from me."

"Did she?"

Carly shrugged. "Sometimes. But it didn't matter." The only man Carly had ever really loved was
Brand.

"Did you compete with her?"

"I tried so hard not to," she admitted and smiled
wryly. "But she was intimidated, simply by my being
there."

"Her parents couldn't see what was happening?"

"I'm sure they could, but their hands were tied. If
they'd intervened, then Joyce would have had all the
more reason to hate me."

"So you were left to sink or swim," he said dryly.

As he spoke, Carly's fingers playfully tugged at the
coarse hairs on his chest.

"If you don't stop doing that, I won't be responsible for what happens," Brand ground out near her ear.

Carly giggled, releasing the tension that had
stretched between them only seconds before. "That
sounds promising."

"I can offer you a lot more than promises," Brand
mumbled and stopped her fingers, capturing one arm.
Twisting, he repositioned himself so that he was
holding her hands down at either side of her head.
"Do you surrender?"

"Never," Carly said and laughed softly. "I'd be
crazy to give up when I'm winning."

"Winning?" he asked incredulously.

"You bet." She lifted her head just enough to press her mouth lightly to his. In a short, teasing action her tongue moistened his mouth. The tips of her unrestrained breasts, through the nylon gown, brushed against his bare chest.

Brand released a short sigh and melted against her. His hands no longer pinned her to the bed as they sought softer, more feminine areas. Carly wasn't given the opportunity to move as his mouth ravaged hers. Pressing her into the mattress, he buried his face in the hollow of her throat, teasing her with his tongue.

"See?" she whispered happily. "What did I tell you? I'm winning."

"You're mighty brave in my mother's house." Brand knew how uncomfortable she'd be making love with only a thin wall separating them from Kay.

"Wait until you see how bold I can get!" Carly said with a soft, subdued laugh.

"Daddy?"

The sound of the soft voice startled Carly. Brand rolled aside and Carly sat upright.

"I can't sleep." Sara stood in the doorway, tightly clutching the blue Smurf under her arm.

"Did we wake you up?" Carly wanted to know, tossing Brand an accusing glare.

"No. I had to go potty and then I heard you giggle and I wanted to giggle, too."

Carly motioned with one finger for Sara to come to her. The little girl scooted eagerly across the floor to Carly's side of the bed. Leaning over, she whispered in Sara's ear and the child broke out in delighted laughter.

"What'd you say about me?" Brand demanded mockingly.

"How'd you know I said anything that had to do with you?"

"You had that look in your eye."

Carly threw back the sheets and Sara crawled under the covers with her. "You can't blame me if women often react to you with laughter. Isn't that right, Sara?"

The little girl agreed with an eager nod.

"What's all the noise about?" Shawn stood in the doorway, rubbing his eyes.

"Did your father wake you up, too?" Carly asked.

"No, Sara did. She was giggling."

"That was Carly," Brand corrected.

Shawn hesitated. "How come Sara gets to sleep with you?"

"That wasn't my idea," Brand said, and lifted the covers. "Might as well let the whole family in here."

Shawn climbed in beside his father. "I'm sleepy. Good night," he whispered.

Brand looked at Carly, with Sara snuggled close in her arms, and the tenderness in his eyes was enough to make her want to cry.

"Good night, family," Brand issued softly and reached for Carly's hand.

Chapter Eleven

The float plane veered to the left after taking off from Dutch Harbor. The small settlement was in the long tail of the Aleutian Islands, which stretched like a graceful arc of stepping-stones between two continents. The Aleutians extended for hundreds of miles to the farthest western extension of North America. Carly gazed out of the window at Unalaska Island, which was wedged between the frigid North Pacific and the storm-tossed Bering Sea.

June had arrived, and Alaska had shed its cold winter coat, stretching and waking to explode in flowers and sunshine. To Carly, with Brand at her side, it was paradise.

She had only flown with him a handful of times, and usually on short trips that were accomplished in less than a day. Now, high above the dark waters, she was amazed by the harshness of the terrain below. The islands had few trees, all of stunted growth. Grass grew in abundance and covered the ground. The contrast with the magnificent cliffs and the forests thick with life on the Alaska mainland was striking.

Looking around her now, she was struck again by the serene mountains. Capped with snow, they stretched for miles in a land called "America's Siberia." Brand had explained that the Aleutian Islands contained the longest range of active volcanoes in the United States. Forty-six was the number he'd quoted her.

Brand turned his attention from the controls. "You're very quiet," he said above the roar of the engine. Reaching for Carly's hand, he kissed her fingertips.

She offered him a dry smile.

"Are you tired?"

"Not at all. I'm overwhelmed by Alaska's diversity." What she was really thinking was how much she wanted Brand to teach her to fly. His reluctance was more obvious every time she brought up the subject. Carly didn't kid herself. She knew why.

"Dutch Harbor's got quite a history," Brand remarked. "During World War II, when Japan was preparing for the battle of Midway, they bombed Dutch Harbor."

"Did their bombers fly off course?" Carly teased. "Midway's in the *South* Pacific."

"No, they'd hoped to draw the Pacific fleet north. The United States spent fourteen months and hundreds of lives in liberating the islands. Most of those men never saw the enemy. They died from the weather and disease.''

Carly's mind filled with images of young men bloody, shaking and freezing. She recalled having read something about the war in the Aleutians.

"How long before we arrive at Lake Iliamna?" She wanted to direct her thoughts from the unpleasant paths her mind was exploring.

"Not long. Are you anxious for our honeymoon?"

"What I want to know is what you had to promise George for me to get all this time off. I thought he'd explode because I wanted to attend Diana's wedding. Now he's given me time off two weeks running.''

"What makes you think I promised him anything?"

"I know George." In some ways she knew him better than she did Brand.

His gaze roamed possessively over her face. "Don't ask so many questions."

Carly had faced a lot of unanswered questions this past week. Brand's children were beautiful, delightful. But she couldn't look at them without seeing Sandra. Brand knew that, and had tried in some illogical way to make it up to her all week. His mother had reminded Carly forcefully that she would never fit into Kay's image of a wife and mother. For a time Carly might be able to fool herself, but it wouldn't last long. She was an intruder in their lives, just as she had infringed on other lives as a child. There were no dreams for her. Only the borrowed ones of others.

Brand had sensed her qualms. All week he'd been watching, waiting. For what, Carly wasn't sure. He might have thought she was going to leave him, but she wasn't. At night, he'd reach for her. "I love you, Carly," was all he'd say. Their lovemaking was volcanic; Brand was rougher, less gentle than he had been in the beginning. With his arms wrapped securely around her, he fell asleep afterward. Carly wasn't so fortunate. She'd slept fitfully all week, waking in the darkest part of the night that precedes dawn. Often she was up and dressed when Brand awoke. They were both praying with a desperation born of silent torment that this time alone, this honeymoon, would set things right.

Lake Iliamna was as beautiful as Brand had described. The male proprietor of the log-cabin lodge welcomed them like family. He'd known Brand since childhood—which meant he'd known Sandra, as well.

Carly tried not to think about that as they climbed the polished stairs that led to their suite. The honeymoon suite.

The moment the door closed, Brand reached for her and kissed her hungrily. His mouth lingered to tease the curve of her lips, brushing over their outline with his tongue.

"Carly," he whispered as he lifted the thick Indian sweater over her head. "I need you." His fingers hurried with the buttons of her blouse, pushing it from her shoulders.

Carly's fingers were just as eagerly working at his clothing, and when they fell into the bed, she kissed him and whispered, "I do love you, Brand." Her voice was small and filled with emotion.

"I know." The desperate ring of his response spoke of his own fears. As if afraid he had admitted something he shouldn't have, Brand kissed her. The hard pressure of his mouth covered hers as he pushed her deep into the comfort of the mattress. When he descended to kiss her breasts, Carly lost herself in the golden sensations of his lovemaking.

Carly stood in her silk robe, gazing out of the window onto the serene, blue lake in the distance. Brand continued to sleep peacefully, undisturbed by her absence. She turned and studied him for an instant as she tried to swallow back the doubts that reared up to face her like a charging enemy. After they'd made love, Carly had lain in his arms and thought how much simpler life would be if she had become his lover instead of his wife. Shawn and Sara were due to arrive in Anchorage in less than two weeks and she wasn't ready. Not emotionally. Not in any way that mattered. These two wonderful children expected a mother...a family—not some emotionally insecure little girl who was struggling to reconcile her past. Shawn, Sara and Brand deserved much more than what she could give them. At least, what she was capable of giving them now.

"Morning." Brand joined her at the window, slipping his hands around her slim waist. His mouth came down to lightly claim her lips and nibble on their softness.

"Why didn't you wake me?" His warm breath mingled with hers.

Carly wrapped her arms around his neck and tried to respond, but her body refused to relax.

"Honey, what's wrong?" His hands rubbed her back in a soothing, coaxing motion as his eyes lovingly caressed hers.

Whenever Brand called her by that affectionate term, she bristled and wanted to scream at him. "Don't call me that," she returned stiffly, hating herself for being so petty.

"'Honey'? Why not?"

Carly inhaled sharply. "Because that's what you used to call Sandra."

The morning light accentuated the frustrated, tired look in Brand's dark eyes. He released her and walked to the other side of the room. Jerking his hand through his hair, Brand expelled a hard breath. "Yes, sometimes I did. But that was then. You're now. Sandra has no part in our lives."

"But ultimately she affects us."

"Carly," he cried, his fists clenched as he struggled to control his anger. "Sandra is *gone.* How long are you going to compete with a dead woman?"

Her arms cradled her stomach as she turned from him and stared sightlessly out the window. Arguing the matter was useless. Her heart was breaking. She couldn't let them continue as they had this week— stepping around one another, avoiding confrontations, pretending nothing was wrong. "I should never have married you, Brand. We would've been wonder-

ful lovers.'' Her voice became a low, aching whisper.
''But what we have now isn't going to work.''

''I don't accept that. You're my wife and I won't let
you go.''

''You'll have to,'' she said gently, hating the emotion that moistened her eyes. ''It isn't in me to let
Shawn and Sara arrive feeling the way I do.''

''They're coming and there's nothing that can be
done about it now.'' Grim anger thinned his mouth
and the sight of it slashed at her conscience. Her heart
cried in anguish, but for a moment no sound came
from the tight muscles of her throat.

''Do you think I enjoy feeling like this?'' she cried
with a flash of hurt and anger. ''I'd give anything to
be different. Shawn and Sara are beautiful, warm
children. But they're *Sandra's* children.''

''They're our children,'' he shouted.

''Then why do I see Sandra every time I look at
them?''

''Because that's all your self-pity allows you to see.
If you'd look past your own insecurities, you'd recognize how much they want and need you. All three of
us do, Carly.'' The desperate edge to his voice in-
flicted another kind of pain. ''Sandra has nothing to
do with us,'' he said in a pleading voice.

''Then you can't recognize what's right in front of
your eyes,'' she accused, fighting back the bitterness.
''What makes you so uncomfortable about me learning to fly?''

Dark eyes narrowed harshly. ''It's dangerous and
any one of a hundred things could happen....''

"And I could be killed," she finished for him. "Sandra died and you're afraid I will, too."

"All right," he shouted. "But what's wrong with being cautious? If I lost you, it'd kill me. If you blame Sandra for that, you're right."

"But where does it stop? Will you be afraid to let me climb or hike or anything else?" She didn't wait for him to respond. "I'm my own person and there will be lots of things I'm going to try."

"I just don't want you to do anything dangerous."

Carly fought to remain outwardly calm and controlled, but the battle was a losing one. "Because of Sandra," she repeated.

"Yes, dammit. I've already lost one wife."

"Brand," she murmured softly, "I can't take that kind of protective suffocation."

He began pacing the floor, clenching and unclenching his fists. The anger exuded from him with every step. Irritation and bewilderment produced a deep frown in his troubled features, but when he spoke his voice displayed no emotion. "I think I knew this was coming," he murmured, his voice thick with resignation. "You haven't been the same since we got back from Portland."

"Your mother is a very perceptive woman. She knew instantly that I wasn't the right kind of wife for you. And certainly not the kind of mother Shawn and Sara need."

"My mother knows nothing." Brand hurled the words at her viciously. He turned and stormed across the room, dressing quickly. His hand was already on the doorknob when he paused and turned to Carly.

"And you know nothing. Go ahead and run. See how far you get. I won't let go of you, Carly. You're my wife and I intend to stay married to you the rest of my life." He left then, leaving Carly standing at the window feeling more wretched and miserable than she could ever remember.

The remainder of their honeymoon was a nightmare for Carly. They barely spoke to one another, and when they did, it was in stilted, abrupt sentences.

On the flight back to Anchorage, neither of them said a word. The lush green beauty of the world below was overshadowed by the heaviness in their hearts.

Brand carried their suitcases up to the apartment and paused inside the door. Silently, he carried Carly's luggage into the bedroom while she shuffled through the mail and noted that there was a long letter from Jutta. They corresponded often now. Carly felt she had gained a valued friend in the older woman. From that first stilted meeting at the correctional center, their relationship had flowered through the mail. Carly was often surprised at how articulate Jutta could be. She was often insightful and wise.

Brand hadn't said a word as they'd entered the apartment. She tried to remain unaffected by his attitude, but she was having trouble succeeding. He'd been cold and distant since that first morning. Not that she blamed him.

Brand sat on the sofa, and when Carly chanced a glance at him, she noted the deeply grooved sadness in his eyes. Part of her yearned to go to him and erase the tension. She'd give anything to be different. Then he raised his gaze to hers and their dark eyes clashed. His narrowed and hardened, as if anticipating a battle. Rising, he moved to his luggage. "I'm going to the house. Until you've settled things within yourself, I'll be there."

"Maybe...maybe that would be for the best," she said evenly. "What about the children? They'll be arriving soon."

A thick brow quirked with mockery. "Why should you care?"

"Because it's only natural that I do. It wouldn't be fair for them—"

"Can't you accept them for who they are?" Brand demanded suddenly, cutting her off.

Carly went white. "Don't you realize how miserable I am over this whole situation?" she shouted, fighting back the tears. "This horrible guilt is eating me alive." Somehow she realized that no amount of arguing would adequately explain her feelings. Nothing she could say would help him understand.

Brand bent down and picked up a suitcase. His face darkened with pent-up emotions. "I have two beautiful children. I'm tired of making excuses for them. And yes," he said, inhaling sharply, "they look exactly like Sandra."

Shock froze her for an instant at the deliberate pain he was inflicting. "You don't need to make excuses for Shawn and Sara," she said urgently, "you just don't understand what—"

"You're right," he interrupted in a hard, cold voice. "I *don't* understand." He turned, and a moment later the front door slammed shut.

Stunned, Carly stood as she was for what seemed an eternity. The hand she ran over her face was shaking uncontrollably. Brand was right, so very right. He should never apologize for children like Shawn and Sara. She moved into the kitchen and put hot water on to boil for coffee. Standing at the counter, her fingers gripped the edge until she felt one long nail give way under the punishing pressure.

"Carly, what's wrong? You never phone during prime time."

"Nothing," Carly lied on a falsely cheerful note. "I'm just calling to see if you're pregnant yet."

Diana laughed with the free-flowing happiness that had echoed in her voice from the moment she'd announced that she was going to marry Barney. "Not yet. But not from lack of trying. What about you and Brand?"

"No." The strangled sound was barely recognizable.

A short silence followed. "Are you going to tell me what's wrong or not?"

Carly choked on a sob. "It's not going to work with Brand and me."

"What do you mean, it's not going to work?" Diana sounded incredulous.

"We aren't living together anymore. Brand moved into the house this weekend. I'm still here at my apartment." Holding the phone to her ear with her shoulder, Carly wiped the tears from her face with both hands. Tilting her head back, she stared blankly at the ceiling light. "I've gone over it a thousand times in my mind. I should never have married him. I can't be the right kind of mother for his children."

"Sweetie, listen to me," Diana said softly in the motherly tone Carly alternately loved and hated. But she needed it now more than she ever had in her life. "You haven't been married a month. Even my first two marriages lasted longer than that. If you love him and Brand loves you, then things will work themselves out. Trust me."

Attempting a laugh that failed miserably, Carly sniffled. "I wish it was that easy."

"Listen, sweetie, it's plain to me that we aren't going to be able to settle this over the phone. I've been looking for an excuse to visit you . . ."

"Diana—no. You can't do that," Carly said urgently, and sniffled again.

"Wild moose won't keep me away. I'll let you know later when my plane's scheduled to arrive."

Carly tried to argue Diana out of a wasted trip. Diana wasn't going to be able to do or say anything to change things. But in the end she resigned herself to the fact that, once Diana had made up her mind about something, it would take more than a few words to change it.

A half hour after talking to Diana, Carly parked her car in the driveway behind Brand's. Her fingers clenched unmercifully around the steering wheel as she gathered her resolve.

The first knock against the door was tentative.

"Come in."

Brand was painting the living room. Newspapers littered the carpet as he spread the antique-white latex color along the neglected walls. Carly recalled choosing this shade for its brightening effect. His roller hardly paused as Carly walked through the door.

"What do you want?"

She died a little at the cold, unfriendly tone of his voice. "I thought I should help. It's...it's only right." Every day brought them closer to the time when Shawn and Sara would be arriving.

"What's right is having you live in this house with me as my wife," Brand returned bitterly. "If you want to do anything to help, then do that."

"I...I can't."

Brand didn't even hesitate. "Then get out."

Shocked at the vicious anger in his voice, Carly was frozen.

"Go on," he repeated.

Hanging her head, Carly closed her eyes against the rush of pain. "I know how irrational I seem," she said in a voice that was barely above a whisper. "And I realize you must be having a hard time believing this, but I love you."

Brand's grunt was filled with sardonic amusement. "Sure you do. If telling yourself that helps soothe your conscience, you keep right on believing it."

"Can't we talk without fighting anymore?" she asked in a tired voice.

Brand tipped his head to one side and arched his thick brows mockingly. "I don't know—can we?"

Carly bristled. She wouldn't be provoked into an argument, and that was clearly what Brand wanted. "Are you going to answer every one of my questions with ones of your own?"

"Why not?" Brand was unhesitating. "I've been facing lots of questions lately."

Shock drained the blood from her face so quickly that Carly thought she might faint. Every foster home, every family she'd ever known had been the same. Just when it seemed that she had finally found a place where she belonged—where she could fit in with a family—it would happen. Something would come about and she'd be sent away. Then everything she had worked to build up would be washed out from under her and she'd be forced to start again. She didn't want it to happen this time. She desperately wanted things to work out. But already Brand was willing to send her out of his life.

With her hands folded primly in front of her, Carly watched him silently as he worked. Even strokes spread the paint across the flat surface. Finally, she gathered enough courage to begin again.

"Diana's coming."

Brand paused in the middle of a downward sweep of the roller and turned around. "Are you running back to Seattle?"

"No." The thought of leaving Brand and the children was intolerable. "She's coming because she wants to talk some sense into me."

Brand turned back to the wall. "I wish her luck. God knows, I've tried."

"Don't you think I know how unreasonable I sound?" Carly shot back angrily. "But it's not reason I *feel*. It's emotion. Is it so wrong to want to be a man's first wife? If that makes me sound selfish and childish, then I agree—that's exactly what I am. All my life I've accepted someone else's leftovers. It's the one thing—the only thing—I didn't want in a husband."

If she expected a reaction from Brand, he gave her none. With his back to her, he continued painting. Carly stood the grating silence as long as she could, then moved to the bedroom that was to be Sara's. Brand had already finished painting it a lovely shade of pink, but the windows were bare, as were those in the freshly painted blue bedroom across the hall. Everything was ready for Shawn and Sara. Everything except Carly.

Diana arrived two days later. Carly met her at the airport and hugged her tightly, holding back the tears.

"Dear Lord, girl, you look terrible."

"That's what you said the last time you saw me," Carly admonished. Heaven knew she couldn't look any worse than she felt. "I don't suppose Barney was thrilled to have you come."

"Barney sends his love. Don't worry about him." Diana put her arm around Carly's waist. "Now, let's get out of here before you burst into tears in the airport."

Carly felt she was ready to do exactly that. She hadn't seen Brand in two days. If *she* wasn't running, he was. Twice she'd gone over to the house, and both times he was nowhere to be seen. No doubt he was in the air, working twice as many hours as any other man.

She doubted that he even knew or cared that she'd been to the house. On her first visit, she'd put up priscilla curtains in Sara's room and made up her new bed with percale sheets printed with Smurf characters. The choice for Shawn's room hadn't been as easy, but she'd chosen drapes with *Star Wars* figures, and a matching bedspread.

In her wanderings around the house Carly had avoided the bedroom she'd once shared with Brand, but had ventured into the kitchen. Neatly washed dishes were stacked on the counter to dry. Brand's efficiency reminded her that he didn't need her to keep his home. He would be fine without her.

"It really is lovely in this part of the world," Diana was saying as Carly's thoughts turned from Brand.

"I told you it was." Her words sounded weak and emotionless even to her own ears.

Carly put on water for coffee when they arrived at the apartment. Her shoulders drooped as she closed her eyes and pressed her lips together.

"Are you sure you're not pregnant?" Diana asked softly. "I can't remember you ever being so pale."

A cold feeling washed over her. For one crazy second she faced contradictory emotions. One part of her felt a rush of excitement, while another experienced a deep sense of dread. Adding a child to this situation would only complicate their problems.

"Carly?" Diana prompted her gently.

"No," she said and swallowed. "There's no possibility of that." She brought down two ceramic mugs from the cupboard and added the dark coffee crystals. When the teapot whistled, she poured the liquid into the mugs. All of her movements were automatic.

As she delivered the steaming coffee to the kitchen table, Diana's eyes studied her carefully. "I've known you from the time you were an adolescent, Carly. I've witnessed these inner struggles of yours for years." Her hand reached across the table and patted Carly's. "Sweetie, isn't it time to bury the hurts of the past and move on?" Her wide-eyed gaze sought Carly's colorless face.

With her head bowed, Carly stared into the dark liquid. "He loved her so much." Her voice was trembling.

"But now Brand loves you."

"He still loves her, and she's standing between us like a steel wedge."

"Only because you see it that way. Won't you give Brand the right to have loved Sandra? He shared lots of years with her, and lots of memories. Are you trying to take that away from him, too?"

"Too?"

"He thinks that what you want is for him to give up his children," Diana declared with a faint note of censure.

"How could he think that? I'd never, never," she repeated forcefully, "ask Brand to do anything of the sort—"

"But he doesn't know that."

Suspicions mounted within Carly. Diana seemed to know far too much about Brand's thoughts to be guessing. "How do you know all this? This has got to be more than speculation on your part."

Diana's gaze didn't flicker. "I talked to him a while ago."

"When?" Carly demanded in a shocked tone.

"Right after I talked to you. He phoned me, Carly. You've got him so twisted up inside he doesn't know what to do. He loves you, but he loves his children, too. Brand seems to think that if he were to have one of his brothers raise Shawn and Sara, then you'd be satisfied.''

Carly's widened gaze sought Diana's face as any icy chill attacked her heart. ''That's not it.''

''I tried to assure him it wasn't.''

The palms of her hands cradled the hot mug until her flesh felt hot and uncomfortable. ''What's wrong with me, Diana? Why am I like this?'' Tears clouded her vision. ''Why can't I thank God that someone as wonderful as Brand loves me?''

''I don't know, sweetie. I don't know.'' Carly's sadness was echoed in Diana's low voice.

Carly paced her bedroom floor that night, unable to sleep. She couldn't remember the last time she'd eaten a decent meal. Diana had been adamant. She seemed to think that a ready-made family was just the thing Carly needed. Carly had almost laughed. A family, *this* family terrified her. She couldn't take Sandra away from the children, and she couldn't separate the children from Brand. There was no solution.

Diana was up before Carly the next morning. ''How'd you sleep?'' she asked.

''Fine,'' Carly lied. Exhaustion reduced her voice to a breathless whisper.

''Little liar,'' Diana murmured.

Carly went into the bathroom, avoiding her friend as she dressed for work. The sound of frying bacon filled the small apartment and Carly had no sooner vacated the bathroom when Diana came rushing in, looking pale and sickly.

Surprised, Carly watched as her friend lost her breakfast. When Diana was finished, Carly handed her a wet washcloth. "You okay?" she asked with a worried expression.

Diana took a couple of deep breaths. "I'm wonderful."

"You are pregnant!"

"I guess so. I had my suspicions, but I wasn't sure." She laughed lightly. "But I am now."

"Congratulations." Carly's voice was softly disturbed. "You should be home with Barney, not in Alaska."

"It won't be any big surprise. Barney guessed last week."

"But you should see a doctor, and the sooner the better."

"I will," Diana's soft laugh was filled with happiness. "As soon as I get back to Seattle."

"Which will be today, if I have anything to say about it. The last thing I need is a pregnant woman on my hands." Carly was teasing her friend affectionately. Diana's life was so perfect. Barney's love had made her friend complete. No one would recognize the Diana of only a year ago in the softly radiant woman she was now. Love had done that for her.

But in Carly's instance, love had created dark shadows under her eyes. It had left her restless and sleepless until exhaustion claimed her in the wee hours of the morning.

Carly held back the tears when she dropped Diana off at the airport later that day.

"I don't think I've done anything to help you, but this is something you've got to settle within yourself," Diana said as she embraced her before boarding her flight.

"I know." Carly swallowed back the emotion building in her throat.

"Be happy," Diana murmured with tears glistening in her eyes. "Don't let the past rob you of the best thing to come along in your life."

Carly couldn't answer with anything but an abrupt shake of her head.

"Keep in contact now, you hear?"

Again Carly nodded. She waited until the plane had made its ascent into the welcoming blue sky before she wiped the moisture from her ashen cheek and headed back to the office.

When she pulled up in front of Alaska Freight Forwarding, the first thing Carly noted was that Brand's car was parked outside. Her heart raced with a thousand apprehensions. Starved for the sight of him, Carly hurried inside, afraid she'd miss him if she didn't move quickly enough.

"Brand." She couldn't disguise the breathless quality in her voice.

He turned, and the stark anger in his eyes stopped her.

"Carly," George stepped around from his desk. "Welcome the newest employee to our firm. You didn't think I'd give you all those days off without compensation, did you?"

Chapter Twelve

"You're working here?" The question managed to make it past the lump of shock that tightened Carly's throat. From the time she'd first started at Alaska Freight Forwarding, George had been trying to get Brand to become a full-time pilot for the company. But the money he made free-lancing his services to the various businesses around town was far and above what he would make flying with one company. That Brand would agree to such an arrangement jolted Carly. And he'd done it so they could visit Portland and Lake Iliamna. She had no doubt that he now considered both those trips wasted in light of what had followed.

"Carly." Brand's greeting was stark.

"Hello." She didn't trust her voice beyond the simplest welcome.

A perplexed expression skirted its way across George's wrinkled face. "Yes, well, it seems you two have several things to discuss." He glanced uneasily from Brand to Carly. "I'll be in the garage."

She waited until the door clicked shut. "Why didn't you tell me?" she asked in a soft, disturbed voice.

Brand gave an aloof shrug, glancing at the clipboard that contained the flight schedule for the week. "It didn't seem important at the time."

She turned her hurt, questioning eyes to his. "Diana and I had a long talk—"

"Obviously it didn't make a hell of a lot of difference," he cut in sharply. "Otherwise your things would be at the house where they belong."

Carly ignored the cold censure in his voice. The lines about his mouth were tight and grim and seemed to be permanently impressed in his rugged features. She remembered that the grooves had relaxed when he'd held her in his arms and they'd made love. She closed her eyes against an unexpected surge of guilt and self-derision. Unwilling for Brand to see the pain he could inflict, Carly lowered her eyes and pretended an acute interest in the correspondence on her desk.

"Diana said you phoned her." She spoke after a few moments.

Dark eyes blazed for an instant, and Carly realized she'd said the wrong thing. He hadn't wanted her to know that he'd contacted her friend.

"I'm glad that you did, because I want to clear away a few misunderstandings."

"Such as?" He set the clipboard aside and poured himself a cup of coffee. Lifting the glass pot up to her, he mutely inquired if she wanted a cup.

Carly shook her head. The only thing she wanted was for them to come to some understanding about their marriage and the children.

Brand took a sip of hot coffee. "You said something about misunderstandings," he prompted.

"Yes." Carly swallowed and moistened her suddenly dry lips. "It's about Shawn and Sara."

Brand's dark features were unreadable as he leaned against the side of George's wooden desk. "The kids are my problem." Heavy emphasis was placed on the fact that he now considered the children his, when once he'd insisted that they were theirs. His words slashed at her heart. His attitude was the result of her craziness, and who could blame him?

"But . . . I'm your wife and . . ."

Brand's snicker was loud enough to make her hesitate. "My *wife?* Are you, Carly? Really?" he taunted, and turned abruptly toward the door. The knob clicked as he turned it. "My impression of husbands and wives was that they lived together. But then, I've been known to be wrong."

Carly bit into her lip to hold back a sob. Brand was lashing out at her in his anger, inflicting pain because he was hurting. Without another word to delay him, Carly stood at the window to watch him leave. He was heading for the airport. A glance at the clipboard confirmed that he'd be flying to Fairbanks. If there was any consolation to Brand being on the payroll, it was that at least now she'd know where he was and when to expect him back. But the solace that offered was little.

Carly purposely stayed late that night, waiting until Brand had checked in with George. She wasn't looking for another confrontation, just the assurance that he'd returned safely. Immediately, it became apparent that having Brand work for the same company had as many drawbacks as advantages. In some ways she'd rather not know his schedule. Ignorance was bliss when she didn't realize he was overdue. Now it would be there for her to face every minute of every day.

The thought of returning to a lonely apartment held no appeal, so Carly decided to take a short drive. Almost without realizing it, she found herself turning the corner that led to the house. Her heart leaped to her throat when she noticed that Brand had installed a swing set in the side yard.

A chill raced up her spine as she parked alongside the curb and examined the polished metal toy. The swings were painted in a rainbow design, with racing stripes wrapped around the poles. Without much imagination Carly could picture two pairs of blue eyes sparkling with happy surprise.

When her gaze slid away from the swing set, she saw that Brand was standing in front of the wrought-iron gate, studying her.

"Was there something you wanted?" he asked coolly.

A sad smile touched the fullness of her soft mouth. "I see that you've risked bribing their affection with a swing set." She was reminding him of his mother's comment.

Their eyes met, and for a flickering moment amusement showed in his glance. "I saw the drapes. When did you bring those over?"

Looking away, Carly avoided the probing intensity of his gaze. "A few days ago."

"Would you like to see what else I've done?"

Her nod was eager. If they talked, maybe Brand would come to understand her doubts. Maybe together they could find a solution. If there was one.

He walked around the car and held open her door for her. When she climbed out, his hand cupped her elbow. The gesture of affection was an unconscious one; Carly was sure of that. But whatever his reason, or lack of it, she couldn't remain unaffected by his touch. A warmth spread its way up her arm. Brand had initiated her to the physical delights of married life, and after only a few days without him, she discovered that she missed his touch. She hungered for the need in his eyes when he reached for her and pulled her into his embrace. At night the bed seemed cold and lonely. She found that she tossed around in her sleep in an unconscious search for her husband.

Brand held open the screen door, allowing Carly to enter ahead of him. A small gasp of surprise escaped before she could control it. New furniture graced the family-size living room. A davenport and matching love seat were the pair they'd talked about purchasing from a local store. Carly had liked the set immensely, but they'd decided to wait until they bought a house before purchasing expensive furniture.

"You decided to go ahead and get the set," she stated unnecessarily. Another armchair was angled toward the fireplace. Carly had teased Brand about buying a chair that made up into a single bed. In discussing the purchase, she'd suggested that they try it out first by making love on it some night in front of a flickering fire.

The look in Brand's eyes confirmed that he remembered her idea. His hands moved to rest on either side of her neck. Carly closed her eyes at the pressure of his thumbs on her collarbones as he erotically massaged her tender skin.

"Isn't the carpeting new, too?" She fought to keep her voice level and so not betray what the gentle caress of his fingers was doing to her.

"Yes," he muttered, dropping his hands.

Carly relaxed and released an unconscious sigh. She couldn't understand why Brand was making so many expensive changes in a rental house. He must have read the question in her eyes.

He turned away from her and ran a hand through his hair, mussing the smooth surface. "When you liked the house so much, I made inquiries about buying it."

Carly nearly choked on a sob. He had done this for her. The irony of the situation produced a painful throb in the area of her heart. Brand was offering her the first home she'd ever known, and she was walking away from him. "You're buying the house? Why?"

He didn't answer her for several long moments. "Anchorage is my home now. Everything I want in life is here. Or soon will be," he amended. "I'm no longer running from the past."

The implication that she still was coated his voice. She wanted to beg him to give her more time to reconcile herself to the fact that she couldn't be his first love. That the children she'd be raising were those of another woman. And again...again, as she had all her life, she would be living on borrowed dreams. Her eyes begged him not to tell her how unreasonable she was being. She already knew. She couldn't hate herself any more than she did at that moment.

"The carpet's beautiful," she murmured. Her gaze drifted past Brand into the cheery kitchen. The room had been repainted a brilliant yellow. He didn't need to tell her that he'd done that for her, too. Once, a few weeks ago, she'd explained that she felt a kitchen should reflect the sunshine. Brand had teased her at the time, commenting that they had enough painting to do. Maybe in a couple of months they'd get around to that. As it was, they'd barely have enough time to prepare the house before Shawn and Sara arrived.

A sob jammed her throat, making speech impossible. Tears blurred her vision. Brand must have seen her reaction to the house and all he'd done. When he reached for her, she went willingly into his arms. His broad chest muffled her sudden tears. Everything she'd ever wanted was here with Brand, but she couldn't accept it. *Home. Family. Love.* The ache in her heart was so profound that she felt like a wounded animal caught in a crippling trap. Only in her case, the trap was of her own making. She couldn't stay. She couldn't go.

"Carly," Brand whispered, and a disturbing tremor entered his voice. He paused to brush the wet strands of hair from her cheek. "Don't cry like that."

Her shoulders shook so hard that catching her breath was nearly impossible. She gasped and released long, shuddering sobs as she struggled to regain her composure. "Hold me," she pleaded in a throbbing voice. "Please, hold me."

His arms came around her so tightly that her ribs ached. Carly didn't mind. For the first time in weeks, she felt secure again. His chin rested on the top of her head until her tears abated. Not until her breathing became controlled and even did she realize that, all the while she'd been weeping, Brand had been talking to her in soothing tones, reassuring her of his love.

"Are you okay?" he asked quietly.

"I'm sorry, so sorry," she murmured over and over. Her sorrow wasn't because of the tears, but because of what she was doing to them both.

In the momentary stillness that followed, Brand allowed a small space to come between them. Her gaze met his penetrating one as he reached out and wiped the moisture from her pale cheek with his index finger. Her lips trembled, anticipating his kiss, and he didn't disappoint her. His mouth captured hers. Warmth seeped into her cold blood at the urgent way in which his mouth rocked over hers.

"Brand." She said his name in a tortured whisper, asking for his love. She needed him. Just for tonight she hungered for the feel of his arms around her, and she longed to wake with him at her side in the morning. Just for tonight, tomorrow, with all its problems, could be pushed aside.

Hugging her more tightly, Brand lifted her into his arms and carried her down the hall and into their bedroom. The springs of the bed made a squeaking sound as he lowered her onto the mattress.

Carly's arms encircled his neck, directing his mouth unerringly to hers. She tasted his restraint the moment his mouth brushed past her lips.

"Brand," she whispered, hurt and confused. "What's wrong?"

He sat on the edge of the bed and leaned forward. The shadow of a dejected figure played against the opposite wall. He looked broken, tired and intolerably sad. Carly propped herself up on one elbow and ran her hand along the curve of his spine. "Brand." She repeated her plea, not knowing what had prompted his actions. She was sure he desired her as much as she did him. Yet he'd called everything to an abrupt halt.

"Before we were married you suggested that we become lovers," Brand began. "I told you then that I wanted more out of our relationship than a few stolen hours in bed." His tone was heavy and tight with the effort it cost him to refuse her. "I married you because I love you and need you emotionally, physically...every way that there is to need another person." He hesitated and straightened slightly. Wiping a hand over his tired eyes, he turned so he could watch her as he spoke. "My home is here—*our* home, our bedroom. I'm asking you to share that with me as your lover, your friend, your confidante, your husband. Someday I want to feel our child growing inside you. I won't accept just a small part of your life. I want it all. Maybe that's selfish of me, but I don't care anymore. All I know is that I can't continue living like this, praying every day you'll see all the love that's waiting for you right here. And worse, witnessing the battle going on inside you and knowing I'm losing. And when I lose, you lose. And Shawn and Sara lose.''

Carly fell back against the mattress and stared at the ceiling. ''Brand, please,'' she pleaded in a soft, pain-filled voice. He couldn't believe that she *wanted* to be like this. She'd give anything to change and be different.

''I'll be your husband, Carly,'' he said flatly, ''when you can be my wife.''

Her heart cried out in anguish, but only a strangled sound came from her throat. Her emotions had been bared and he'd known how desperately she'd needed him. There hadn't been any pretense in her coming to him tonight. She'd wanted his love and he was sending her away.

By some miracle, Carly managed to stumble out of the bedroom and the house. She didn't stop until she arrived back at the apartment. There were no more tears in her to cry as she paced the floor like a caged wild animal confined to the smallest of spaces. Mindless exhaustion claimed her in the early-morning hours, but even then she slept on the davenport rather than face the bedroom alone.

The following morning, Carly was able to avoid seeing Brand. Intuition told her that he was evading her as well.

At the end of what seemed like the longest day of her life, Carly drove to her apartment, parked the car and, without going inside, decided to go for a walk. If she was able to exert herself physically, maybe she'd be tired enough to sleep tonight. With no set course in mind, she strode for what seemed miles. Her hands were buried deep in her pockets, her strides urgent. At every street she watched in amazement as long parades of boys and girls captured her attention. Never had she seen more children. It was the first week of June and the evenings were light. Young boys were playing war in their army fatigues. For a time a small troop followed her, dashing in and out of the bushes along her chosen route. Ignoring them, Carly focused her attention directly ahead until her eyes found a group of young girls playing with cabbage-faced dolls in the front yard of a two-story white house.

Quickening her pace, she discovered that she was near the library. A good book would help her escape her problems. But once inside, Carly learned that the evening was one designated for the appearance of a prominent storyteller. The building was full of children Shawn's and Sara's age. One glance inside and Carly rushed back out. Her breath came in frantic gasps as she ran away.

For one insane moment Carly wanted to accuse Brand of planning the whole thing. She didn't need to be told her thoughts were outrageous, but the realization didn't help cool her indignation.

The remainder of the week passed in a blur. If she was staying away from Brand, then he had changed his strategy and was making every excuse to be near her.

"I don't mind telling you," George commented early Monday morning, "I've been worried about you and Brand. The air between you has seemed a mite thick lately."

Carly ignored him, centering her attention on the Pacific Alaska Maritime docking schedule. "We should get the Wilkens account to Nome by Thursday."

"I was worried," George continued, undaunted, "but the way Brand watches you, I know that what brought you two together is still alive and well." He chuckled and rubbed the side of his unshaven cheek. "On his part, anyway."

Carly's fingers tightened around her pencil. "Have you looked over Primetime Gold's claim for the last shipment? Apparently, the dredging parts were damaged."

If George made one more comment on the way Brand was looking at her, Carly was sure the pencil would snap. Brand came into the office daily when he knew she'd be there. Often he poured himself coffee, looking for an excuse to linger and talk to her. He wasn't exactly subtle with what he had to say.

"Three more days" had been his comment this morning. He didn't need to elaborate. Shawn and Sara would be arriving on Thursday.

"I need longer than that," Carly had pleaded for the hundredth time. "I'm not ready for them. I want to be sure."

The pain in Brand's eyes mirrored her own. "But will you ever know? That's the question. Dammit, Carly, how can you turn away from us when we love and need you?"

"I can't rush what I feel," she murmured miserably.

"If you're waiting for me to give up Shawn and Sara, set your mind straight right now. I won't."

"Oh, Brand," Carly cried softly, then dejectedly lowered her head so that her chin was tucked against her shoulder. "I would never want that."

"Then just what do you want? Three days, Carly," he repeated with grim impatience. "They're arriving in three days, and they expect a home and a mother."

"I won't be there. I can't," she cried on a soft sob.

The pain etched in Brand's eyes as he left the office haunted Carly for the remainder of the day.

George had already left for the afternoon when Brand checked in after a short flight. He filled out the information sheet and attached it to the clipboard for George's signature.

Although Carly attempted to ignore the suppressed anger in his movements, it was impossible. Silently, her eyes appealed to him. His gaze met hers boldly, and darkened.

"If you're through, I'd like to close up," she said, struggling to control the breathless quality in her voice. The office keys were clenched tightly in her hand. She'd seen that look on Brand's face before. Grim anger hardened his eyes to a brilliant shade of brown, wary anger that all but flashed at her.

"Why should your likes concern me? Obviously my needs don't trouble you," he taunted softly. "Carly, I'm tired of playing the waiting game. I want a wife." With every word, he advanced toward her. An unfamiliar hardness stole into his features.

Backed against the wall beside the door, Carly stared at him with wide-eyed shock. This wasn't the Brand she knew and loved, but some wild stranger. A man driven to the limit of his endurance. When he tried to kiss her, she eluded his demanding mouth; her hands strained against his chest as she attempted to twist free.

"What's the matter?" Brand challenged. "I'm only giving you what you wanted so badly the other night."

"No," she cried out with indignation and hurt. "Not like this!"

"Why not?" He pinned her to the wall by weaving his hands into her hair, trapping her. "My patience has run out. If I have to take you by force, then I will. It's what you deserve for putting me through this hell." His mouth curved into a sardonic smile that was almost cruel. Again his mouth sought hers, punishing her with a ruthless kiss that ground his teeth against hers in his savagery.

Carly tried to resist him by jerking her head back and forth, but the pain of his fingers tangling in her hair brought involuntary tears to her eyes. By the time she realized his game, it was too late. She had expended her strength in useless struggles that had only amused him.

When she was weak and panting, he began kissing her. At first he was gentle, his mouth caressing and teasing hers until she responded, wrapping her arms around his neck and arching against him so that her body was intimately thrust against his.

"I should take you here and now," he whispered cruelly, and reached behind her for the zipper of her skirt.

"Brand, no," she pleaded again. "Don't do this. Please, don't do this." She couldn't believe that he'd force her, but she'd never seen Brand like this. To fight his iron grip was useless. He was by far the stronger and seemed determined to humiliate her.

The skirt had twisted its way around her waist and her struggles had only aided its progress. Carly didn't recognize the soft whimpering sounds as her own until Brand paused, his breath harsh against her ear. One hand was painfully crushed against her breast, and slowly he removed it and relaxed his hold, freeing her slightly.

He looked at her with wide, shock-filled eyes, as if he'd just woken from a trance and hadn't known what he'd been doing.

"Are you all right?" His voice was low, and he took a step back.

Hot tears made wet trails down her pale, bloodless face. It took all her energy to nod. A bruise was forming on her shoulder where Brand had forced her against the wall. She could feel it, and, once free, she attempted to rub the ache from it.

If Carly was pale, Brand was more so. He looked for a moment as if he was going to be ill. He hesitated only long enough to jam his shirttails inside his pants.

Without giving her another look, he turned toward the door.

"There was no excuse for that," he said, looking away from her. "It won't happen again."

"Brand..."

Half out the door, he stopped and glanced over his shoulder, but he made no attempt to come to her. His eyes met hers in quiet challenge. There were so many things she wanted to say, but no thought seemed clear in her mind.

"I... I understand," she murmured.

Chapter Thirteen

On Tuesday afternoon, another long letter from Jutta Hoverson was waiting for Carly. She held off opening the envelope until after the water had boiled for her coffee. Carrying the mug to the kitchen table, she sat down and propped her bare feet on the opposite chair.

Of all the people in the world, Carly expected that Jutta would understand the hesitancy she felt toward Brand and the children. Diana, whom she loved and respected, hadn't come close to comprehending the heart-wrenching decision Carly faced. More than once during Diana's short visit, Carly felt that Diana had wanted to give her a hard shake. For once, Carly needed someone to identify with her needs, her insecurities. Jutta could do that.

Slipping the letter from the long envelope, she read:

Dear Carly,

My friend. Your letter arrived today and I've read it many times. You speak of your love for this man you have married. But you say that you are no longer living with him. I don't understand. In your last letter you wrote about his children and I sensed your discontent. You love, yet you fear. You battle against the things in life that are most natural. Reading your letter reminded me of the time when I was a young girl who dreamed of being a great runner. I worked very hard to accomplish this skill. My uncle coached me. And in his wisdom he explained that running demands complete coordination. He said that to be a good runner, I must let everything I'd learned, and everything I knew deep inside, come together and work for me. But I lost every race. Even when I knew I was the best, I couldn't win. Again and again, he said to me that once I quit trying so hard to win, I would. Of course, I didn't understand him at the time. I struggled, driving myself harder and harder. Then, one day at race time, my uncle threw up his hands at me. He said I would never win, and he walked away. And so I decided I wouldn't even try. When the race began, I ran, but every step still felt heavy, every breath an effort. Then something happened that I don't understand even now. Maybe because I wasn't trying, because I no longer cared to win, everything my uncle had tried to explain came

together. My feet no longer dragged and every
step seemed only to skim the surface. I no longer
ran. I flew. I made no effort. I felt no strain. My
rhythm was perfect and I experienced a pure exhilaration and a joy I have never known since. I
won the race and for the only time in my life,
maybe, I made my family proud.

My friend, in many ways we are alike.

Jutta

Carly reread the letter three times. The message
should have been clear, but it wasn't. Jutta had listened to the advice of an uncle and won a race. Carly
couldn't see how that could relate to Brand and the
children. The letter was a riddle Jutta expected Carly
to understand. But Carly had never done well with
word puzzles.

Not until Carly was in bed did she think again of
Jutta's strange letter. The picture her mind conjured
was of a young, dark-hair girl struggling against high
odds to excel. In some ways, Carly saw herself. With
her personality quirks, her chances for happiness had
to be slim. Her thoughts drifted to the first few days
of lightheartedness after she and Brand were married. Content in their love, they had lived in euphoric
harmony.

Suddenly, Carly understood. Abruptly, she struggled to a sitting position and turned on the small lamp
at the side of her bed. This kind of underlying accord
was what Jutta had tried to explain in her letter. There
was harmony in Jutta's steps as she ran because she no
longer struggled. When something is right, really

right, there is no strain, no effort. The harmony of
body and soul supersedes the complications of life.
There were rhythms and patterns to every aspect of
human existence, and all Carly had to do was accept
their flow and move with the even swell of their tides.
Problems erupted only when she struggled against this
harmony. Once she reconciled herself to this flow, she
could overcome the trap of always fearing borrowed
dreams.

Carly didn't know how she could explain any of this
to Brand, but she knew she had to try. The physical
strain that had marked her face over the last weeks relaxed as she dialed the phone. He'd think she was
crazy to be calling him this late at night, particularly
when she didn't know what she was going to say.
Probably the best thing to do was blurt out the fact
that she loved him and that together they'd work out
something. The love they shared was the harmony in
her life because it was right. A lot of uncertainties remained; she hadn't reconciled everything. But at least
now she could see a light at the end of the tunnel.

The phone rang ten times and Brand didn't answer.
Perplexed, Carly replaced the receiver. A look at her
wristwatch confirmed that it was after midnight.
Brand worked hard, and he slept hard. It was possible he'd sleep through the telephone's ringing, but not
likely.

A quick mental review of the week's flight schedule
reminded her that Brand had been flying some Seattle
personnel to one of the Aleutian Islands that day. The
flight was as regular as clockwork. Brand had taken
the same route a thousand times. He hadn't checked

in before she'd left work, she remembered. But then, she'd left a little early. She really didn't have anything to worry about. If something had gone awry with Brand's flight, George would have contacted her.

A long, body-stretching yawn convinced Carly to go back to bed. In the morning she'd make a point of seeking Brand out. Shawn and Sara were due to arrive the day after next, and she was hoping they could talk about that meeting.

Brand's Chevy was parked by the warehouse when Carly arrived at work the following morning. A smile lit up her face at the reassuring sight. Everything was fine.

"Where's Brand?" she asked her boss as she breezed in the door. "I'd like to talk to him before he takes off."

George looked up from the report he was scanning. "He hasn't arrived yet."

Carly shook her head and gave George a bemused grin. Sometimes her boss could be the most forgetful person. "Of course he's here. His car's parked out back."

George glanced up and released an exaggerated sigh. "I tell you, he hasn't come in this morning." Glancing at the thick black watch on his wrist, George's brows rose suspiciously. Brand wasn't in the habit of arriving late.

"What time did he check in last night?" Carly questioned.

With deliberate care, George set the paper he was reading aside. "You tell me. I left early."

Carly discovered that her legs would no longer support her, and she sank into the swivel chair at her desk. "I thought he was checking in with you. I assumed . . ."

"You mean Brand didn't come back to the office yesterday?"

Carly felt her heart sink so low it seemed to land at her ankles. "You mean . . ." She couldn't voice the thought.

"His car's still here. He didn't come back." George finished for her. He stood and grabbed the clipboard that held the flight schedules down from the wall. "Don't panic—everything's going to be fine. There's no cause for alarm." The rising uneasiness in his own voice wasn't reassuring. "I'll contact the airport and confirm his flight plan." George was out the door faster than she had seen him move in three months of working at Alaska.

Numbly, Carly sat. She couldn't have moved to save the world. Constant recriminations pounded at her from all sides until she wanted to bury her head in her hands. This was her fault. If Brand was hurt, no one would ever be able to convince her otherwise. Again and again George had told her that Brand was an excellent pilot. The best. Alaska Freight Forwarding was fortunate to have him on their team. Hiring Brand had been a coup for George.

But even excellent pilots made mistakes. Anyone was more prone toward error when his mind was preoccupied—and God knew that Brand had lots on his mind. He was working hard, and if he was anything like Carly, he hadn't been sleeping well. The combination of hard work and lack of sleep was enough to bring down the best pilots in the business.

When George returned forty-five minutes later, Carly knew her face was waxen. Her eyes searched his eagerly for information.

George cleared his throat, as if reluctant to speak. "There've been screwups everywhere, including the airport. They figure Brand has been missing close to fourteen hours."

"Oh, God." Carly felt as if someone had physically slammed a fist into her stomach. She didn't say anything. The thoughts that flittered through her mind made no sense. She recalled that she had to go pick up some dry cleaning on her way home from work. Then she remembered that Diana had expected something horrible to happen once she'd decided to marry Barney. Happiness wasn't meant for people like her. Nor was it meant for someone like Carly.

"Carly, are you okay?" George was giving her a funny look, and she wondered how long he'd been trying to gain her attention.

"Search and rescue teams are in the air. They'll find him."

Carly was confident they would, sooner or later. The question neither of them was voicing was in what condition Brand would be found: dead or alive.

The entire day was like a nightmare. Only Carly discovered that, no matter what she did, she couldn't wake up. The amount of manpower and man-hours that went into finding a missing or downed pilot was staggering. Reports were coming in to the office from the command center at Anchorage Airport continu-

ally. If that was encouraging, the news wasn't. Brand
hadn't been sighted, and a thick fog was hampering
the search.

At ten that night, George put his hand over Carly's. "You might as well try to get a good night's sleep.
I'll let you know the minute I hear anything."

Carly's answer was an abrupt shake of her head.
"No. I won't leave. Not until I know."

George didn't try to persuade her further. But she
noticed that he didn't leave, either. Both were determined to see this through, no matter what the out-
come.

At some point during the long night, Carly fell
asleep. With her head leaning against the wall, she'd
meant to rest her eyes for only a few minutes, but the
next thing she knew, it was light outside and the sun
was over the horizon. Immediately, she straightened
and sought out George, who shook his head grimly.

Two hours later, with her nerves stretched taut,
Carly forced herself to eat something for the first time
since breakfast the day before. She ran a comb
through her dark hair and brushed her teeth.

George was staring into the empty coffee cup he was
holding when she approached him.

"I don't know when I'll be back."

He looked at her blankly. "Where are you going?"

"To the main terminal. Shawn and Sara are arriving in a half hour. I don't want them to know Brand's
missing. If you hear anything, I'll be at the house."
She let out a tired breath. "I'll try to phone as often
as I can."

Squeezing her numb fingers, George offered Carly a smile and nodded.

It didn't seem possible that a day could be so full of sunshine and happiness—and that Carly's whole world could be dark with an unimaginable gloom.

As the Alaska Airlines flight with Shawn and Sara aboard touched down against the concrete runway, Carly felt an unreasonable surge of anger. Maybe Brand had planned this so she would be forced to deal with his children. If he'd wanted to find a way to punish her, he'd been highly successful.

As the stewardess ushered Shawn and Sara out from the jetway, Carly straightened her shoulders and forced a smile to her dry lips. Her composure was eggshell fragile. She hadn't yet figured out what she was going to say to the children.

"Mom." A brilliant smile lit Sara's sky-blue eyes. She broke free from the young stewardess and hurried toward Carly.

Scooting down, Carly was the wary recipient of a fierce hug from the little girl. Shawn was more restrained, but there was a happy light in his eyes she hadn't noticed during her visit to Oregon.

"Where's Dad?" Shawn was the first to notice that his father was missing.

Not quite meeting his inquisitive eyes, Carly managed a smile. "He told me to tell you how sorry he is that he couldn't meet the two of you today. But he's hoping you like the surprise he has waiting for you at the house."

"Can we go there now?" Sara asked. Her blond hair had been plaited into long pigtails that danced with the action of her head. The blue Smurf doll was clutched under her arm.

"I'll take you there now. Are you hungry?"

Both children bobbed their heads enthusiastically. Rather than find something to cook, Carly located a McDonald's. Shawn and Sara were delighted with the fact that their first meal in Alaska was to be a hamburger and milk shake.

When they reached the house, Shawn helped Carly unload the suitcases from the back of the car. "Grandma sent you a long letter. She said it was instructions."

"Then I should read it right away."

"Don't," Shawn returned soberly. "You can, if you want," he added after a momentary lapse in conviction. "But you don't have to do what she says."

"At least not the nap part. Right?" She gave him a conspiratorial wink.

"Right," Shawn confirmed with a nod.

"Mom, Mom." Sara rushed from her bedroom. "I've got a loose tooth. Look." She started pushing one of her front teeth back and forth. "Does the Tooth Fairy live in Alaska, too?"

"You bet," Carly answered, wiggling the tooth to satisfy Sara.

While Shawn and Sara investigated their new swing set, Carly unpacked their clothes. A quickly placed call to George confirmed that there hadn't been any word. A glance out of the window revealed that both Shawn and Sara had discovered neighborhood children their age.

"This is Lisa." Sara had brought her newfound friend into the house. "Can I show her my bedroom?"

"Go ahead."

Sara looked surprised, as though she'd expected Carly to refuse. "We won't make a mess."

"Good," Carly said with a short laugh. "I'd hate to think of you spending your first day in Alaska cleaning your room."

"Sara's never messy," Shawn said with a soft snicker. "At least, that's what Grandma says."

With a superior air, Sara led her friend down the hall to her bedroom. Lisa gave an appropriate sigh of appreciation at the beauty of the room, which immediately endeared her to Carly.

After the children had settled in, and Sara had taken a short nap, Carly drove them over to the apartment. Every night after work, she'd dreaded coming home. Now she understood the reason. She didn't belong here.

While she packed her things, Carly thought through the sober facts that faced her. Reality said that Brand could be dead. Her heart throbbed painfully at the thought, but it was a fact she couldn't ignore. If so, the question she had to deal with was what would happen to Shawn and Sara. Brand's mother was traveling. Her long vacation was well deserved. Kay St. Clair had done her best for these children, but she'd more than earned a life of her own. The state could remand Shawn and Sara as they had Carly. She'd been five when she'd gone to her first foster home. Sara's tender age.

Carly's fist tightened at the ferocity of her emotion. No matter what it took, she wouldn't allow that to happen. Not to Shawn and Sara. They would be hers, just as if she'd given them life. Nothing would separate the three of them. The path of her thoughts brought another realization. All these weeks that she'd battled within herself, she'd been fighting the even flow of her life's rhythm. It wasn't that she couldn't give Brand something he didn't already have. It was what Brand, Shawn and Sara could give her. Borrowed dreams were irrelevant. What they shared was new and vital. Brand had tried to tell her that in so many ways, and she hadn't understood.

"Mom." Sara stood in the open doorway, giving Carly a puzzled look. "I was talking to you."

Holding out her arms, Carly gave the small child a loving squeeze. "I'm sorry. I was thinking."

"Does thinking make you cry?"

Carly's fingers investigated her own face, unaware that tears had formed. She wiped the moisture from her cheeks and tried to laugh, but the sound couldn't be described as one of mirth. "Sometimes," she said with a sniffle. "Hey, you know what I really need? A big hug." Sweet Sara was eager to comply.

Both children wanted to listen to their favorite story once they returned to the house. Carly promised them a special dinner to go with the book. Somehow, she'd find a way to cook "green eggs and ham." Luckily, neither child seemed to find it out of the ordinary to see Carly move her clothes from one house to another. At least, they didn't mention it. But Carly wouldn't be moving again. Her place was here.

The book was Shawn's favorite Dr. Seuss. The boy sat beside her while Sara occupied Carly's lap. The thought slid through her mind as she opened the book that, although Shawn and Sara resembled their mother, they were amazingly like their father. The curious tilt of Shawn's head was all Brand.

Carly was only a few pages into the book when a movement caught her attention. The front door was open and George stood just outside the closed screen.

A myriad of sensations assaulted Carly. Their eyes met and Carly's clouded with emotion, begging him to tell her everything was all right. Tears blurred his expression. But in her heart she knew the news wasn't good. If Brand had been found alive, George would have phoned.

"You weren't here when I phoned," George said. "But what I have has to be seen."

Carly's arms tightened around the children, drawing them protectively close to her. Again she confirmed the thought that nothing would separate Shawn and Sara from her.

The screen door opened and Carly braced herself.

"Dad." Shawn flew off the love seat.

Carly jerked her head up to find Brand framed in the doorway. He scooped Shawn into his arms and reached down for Sara. Carly remained frozen.

"Mom said she didn't know what time you'd be home."

"Is that right?" Brand said, hugging his children close. "We'll have to make sure Mom knows from now on, won't we?" His eyes sought Carly's, bright with promise. "Isn't that right, Mom?"

"Yes." Carly nodded eagerly and walked into Brand's embrace. "Dear God, what happened? I was worried sick.... I thought I'd lost you forever." She wept into his shoulder, knowing he probably couldn't understand anything she was saying. It didn't matter now that he was here. Not when he was holding her as if his very life depended on it. Later, when the children were in bed, he could fill in the details.

"Mom unpacked all the suitcases," Sara said happily. "Even hers."

Brand relaxed his hold so that he could lift Carly's chin and brush the wet strands of hair from her face. "Are you staying?" The husky question was so low Carly could barely hear him.

"Hey, kids," George said, clearing his throat. "Why don't you two show me your bedrooms? And wasn't that a swing set I saw outside?"

A grateful smile touched Carly's trembling lips as George led the children from the living room.

"I'm never leaving. Oh, Brand, I know it all sounds crazy, but I realize I belong with you. Shawn and Sara are *our* children." She couldn't hide the breathlessness in her voice. "Everything's clear now.... I'm not borrowing anyone else's dreams, but living my own."

Sara skipped excitedly back into the room and squeezed her small body between Brand and Carly. Brand reached down and lifted her up. Two small arms shot out. One went around Carly and the other around Brand. "I'm so glad you're here."

"I'm home now," Brand murmured in a raw, husky voice and his eyes found Carly's. "We're all home."

*   *   *   *   *